BOOTHILL BRAND

Newly arrived in Broken Horn, Frank McLowry soon discovers that any queries relating to his brother Emmet's death are met with indifference or plain hostility. Old Pedro sets him on the trail to Anvil Mesa, and there he finds himself in the middle of a battle of wits and flaming six-shooters. He knows he will have to win if he is to eradicate the Boothill brand, under which he has chosen to ride.

WADE BRONSON

BOOTHILL BRAND

Complete and Unabridged

LINFORD
Leicester

First published in Great Britain in 1993 by
Robert Hale Limited
London

First Linford Edition
published November 1994
by arrangement with
Robert Hale Limited
London

The right of Wade Bronson to be identified
as the author of this work has been asserted
by him in accordance with the
Copyright, Designs and Patents Act, 1988

British Library CIP Data

Bronson, Wade
    Boothill brand.—Large print ed.—
Linford western library
I. Title II. Series
823.914 [F]

ISBN 0–7089–7597–6

Published by
F. A. Thorpe (Publishing) Ltd.
Anstey, Leicestershire

Set by Words & Graphics Ltd.
Anstey, Leicestershire
Printed and bound in Great Britain by
T. J. Press (Padstow) Ltd., Padstow, Cornwall

This book is printed on acid-free paper

1

FRANK McLOWRY had travelled a hundred miles and asked as many questions to find this place. He left his black horse in a small stand of cottonwoods and walked the last twenty yards to the railed-in cemetery, slowing as he neared the forlorn cluster of greyed and lichened tombstones and monuments.

Crimson and orange flecked the late afternoon sky. A wind soughed up over the range grasses and touched his cheeks with the lingering gentleness of a kiss. McLowry dragged his weather-battered stetson from his dark head and entered the plot, aware of the subtle tuggings of many ancient memories.

Emmet's marker was there all right, as the bartender in Broken Horn had said, a square of bleached board that read 'Emmet McLowry — died June 1877.'

McLowry kneeled by the grave and let a host of pent-up feelings breach the tight dam in his chest.

A rustle of sound behind him caused him to rise and swing around with his fingers falling to the .45 Colt holstered on his hip. An elderly Mexican stood there, straw sombrero in hand, veined face giving slow birth to a faint smile.

"He was a good man, señor," he said softly.

McLowry nodded, frowning. His keen eyes searched the old face. His tight mouth relented.

"You knew him?"

"Si. I knew him. I heard you ask questions in town. I followed you to make sure you would find the place. You do not mind? My name is Pedro Juarez."

"Of course not," McLowry said gruffly. "But somebody had different ideas about Emmet."

The faded eyes regarded him intently,

2

speculatively. "That is so, señor. He was killed."

"You know how, *amigo*?"

The Mexican lifted his shoulders in a shrug. "He was shot. In the street of Broken Horn. At night, when the shadows befriended his slayer." He spread talon-like hands. "It is all I know."

"Or are willing to tell?" McLowry regretted the observation almost immediately. Pain clouded the lined face. It resembled seasoned mahogany in the fading sunlight.

"It is all I know, señor."

"Sure." McLowry grunted. "Sorry if I hurt your feelings." He forced a grin. "Well, Pedro, there's nothing to keep me here. It's a place for rest, and I don't intend to do much of that until I find out all there is to know about Emmet's shooting."

"You are like the other one. You were brothers?"

"That's right."

"You are staying in Broken Horn?"

"For the time being. I'm heading back there now."

"I left my mule in the trees."

With a last look at the weather-scoured marker, McLowry strode down the slope, keeping the Mexican in front of him. He felt a qualm of guilt about the precaution, but at this juncture it was impossible to tell friend from foe.

"I am travelling to town, señor."

"Let's go, then."

They set off through the gathering dusk, McLowry holding the pace of his black horse to that of the mule. Pedro Juarez rode in silence, locked in some secret world of his own. He had set out to help the big, craggy-jawed stranger, taken the trouble to follow him out of town, and he had offered his tribute to Emmet. It was a little, and yet it was a lot, and if McLowry could discount the possibility of Juarez acting on someone's orders, it showed that Emmet must have had friends as well as an enemy who hated him deeply enough to kill him.

An hour later the two men parted company at an intersection half way along Broken Horn's main thoroughfare, and with Pedro Juarez's soft "*Adios, amigo,*" in his ears, McLowry took the horse he called Blackie to the livery he had visited earlier in the day. He returned to the street and bent his steps towards the sheriffs office which he had decided to give a wide berth until he had actually seen Emmet's grave.

McLowry strode along like a man with all the time in the world to get to where he was going. He had an odd swing to his shoulders, a noticeable roll to his step. He was a big, stringy, rawboned man with a still face in which restless grey eyes struck a sharp contrast. He was aware of the odd quizzical glance slanted in his direction without betraying the fact.

He knuckle-rapped the open door leading into the musty-smelling dusty office hallway and waited until a dry, rustling voice grudgingly acknowledged his presence.

"Come in."

Sheriff Dan Bennet was a heavily-built man with a blunt face, a somewhat protruding, aggressive chin, and dark eyes that narrowed a trifle at the advent of the newcomer. He started to rise from his chair on McLowry's entrance but then dropped back, deciding the formality was uncalled for.

"Oh, it's you." A crooked smile bent the rather flat, petulant lips. He nodded permission for McLowry to take the chair opposite him. McLowry thumbed his hat-brim up a little and sat down.

"Seems like you might have been expecting me, Sheriff."

"In a way." Bennet was not given to easy admissions. "I expected you like folks expect rain when the clouds darken up." He sighed, plucked a stogie from a vest pocket and rasped a match on the sole of his boot. "Word soon got about that somebody connected with Emmet McLowry had arrived in town. I put my deputy, Jed

Deakin, to watching you. He reported that you trailed your ear around some and then rode out."

McLowry's mouth puckered. "Is that all?"

"Well, I know that old Juarez saddled up his mule and went after you. Did he earn his two bits?"

"As a matter of fact I overlooked paying him off. I'll do it next time I see him, though."

"So you're staying in town?" Bennet tried to make the question casual, but subtlety was not one of his strong points, and McLowry detected an underlying note of anxiety.

"I guess I'll hang around for a while. Unless you've got some objection."

The lawman ignored the irony. "How long do you propose to be around?" he queried.

"Hard to say. Until I sort out a certain matter that's bothered me."

"You don't have to be coy about it, mister. You're referring to the killing of your brother?"

"I take it you might have known him, Sheriff?"

Bennet twitched his shoulders. "I did, and I didn't. Oh, sure, I know just about everybody in town. You can't help tripping over them. That's how you find out about folks. A little bit here, a little bit there. By and by you've got something that might add up."

McLowry had been regarding him with a shadowed brow. "This tripping business; would Emmet have been low enough to the ground to trip over?"

"Take it easy now. Don't get me wrong."

"I just want to get you straight."

Bennet eased himself from his chair, not with the effort of a too-heavy man, but with the litheness of a very fit and ready man. He paced around the desk and stood behind McLowry. And without turning his head McLowry knew he was using the stogie as a pointer.

"I've already indicated that I didn't know a lot about your brother."

"But you *do* know he was my brother?"

"Hell yes. That much is evident. And there's certainly a family resemblance. In fact, I'd say that you were pretty much alike."

"Who killed Emmet, Sheriff?"

The question hung in the air for a while like a dangerous thing which should not be touched. Dan Bennet moved to where he could look his visitor straight in the face.

"I don't know," he answered at length.

"I hope it won't hurt your feelings if I ask if you've tried to find out."

"I've tried to find out, sure. Maybe this sounds old-fashioned, but I take a pride in rodding a clean town. I come down pretty hard on roughnecks, any kind of law-breaker."

"That's all candy I've tasted before, Sheriff." McLowry produced a cigar and placed it between his teeth. His teeth were very white. He rose, pushing his head to within six inches of the

9

office roof. A meagre smile played at the corners of his mouth. "Don't get me wrong, Sheriff. I appreciate everything you say. Thanks for the help."

Dan Bennet let him reach the doorway before informing him in a flat, uncompromising voice: "Remember what I said about a clean town. You'll do that, mister?"

"You bet, Sheriff. So-long."

When McLowry had gone into the thickening gloom the door leading to the cell block swung open and a lanky man emerged. He had a pronounced stoop to his shoulders and his lugubrious expression had long since become a permanent feature. Still, there was a suggestion of slyness, strength and energy about him. He permitted a tentative smile to brighten his narrow-jawed face.

"I knew he'd call," he announced throatily. "What do you think, Dan?"

The question appeared to irritate the sheriff. He studied the tip of his stogie, grimaced as if it had gone sour on him, and went to fling it into the street. "I think we might be in for more trouble than we need," he said when he came back.

"We don't have to wait for it. Think up some charge to throw at him. Say it breaks an ordinance that calls for him to pull his freight."

"Got any bright ideas?"

"The vagrancy law. Give him a couple of days to get a job, then haul him up and tell him to drift."

Bennet went around his desk and sat down. "Not sure that would work, Jed. This McLowry bird is no fool. He looks like he's been kicked in the teeth before today, and he looks like he's done his share of kicking."

"We'll figure out something, Dan," the deputy rejoined confidently.

★ ★ ★

Frank McLowry hunted up a hotel, booked a room, and ate an early supper.

11

The place was well-lighted, and when he had finished his meal he retired to the small parlour where he smoked a cigar. There were some newspapers and periodicals on a table, most of them well-aged and consequently well-thumbed, but he browsed through them for a while. He enjoyed reading when he had a chance to do so, but just then he could manage to concentrate only half of his mind. He was wondering if his coming to Broken Horn would bring any repercussions of significance. It might be like dropping a stone into a still pond, when the ripples might spread and produce some worthwhile result. People — or even someone like Pedro Juarez — who had seen Emmet as a friend, might come forward to help. And if the killer was still in the vicinity, he might be curious enough to approach him, if only to appraise his potential.

At the end of an hour McLowry went into the street. It was now black as pitch. Some of the saloons and gaming houses boasted naphtha flares outside their doors, but these merely accentuated the general darkness. He turned off towards the north end of the town, catching the tang of woodsmoke from chimneys. The scent evoked some pleasant memories — the warm stove in a cheerful bunkhouse on a winter night, with the buzz of friendly chatter, and when the biggest problem on a man's mind was the early start he had to make in the morning; cougar hunts in the high woods with Emmet and the two panting hounds straining on their leashes, camp fires on lonely trails when dawn unfailingly ushered in a new world for a man to ride into. How long ago had all that been — two years, five, a hundred?

Old age overtaking him at last, he reflected whimsically, if thirty-five could be called old. Still, a man could pack a lot of living and experience into thirty-five years, most of which had been spent in the open, shifting from range to range, from job to job. Trail-herder, cowpoke, horse-wrangler, bartender — for three months when he was right down on his luck — and which occupation had ended in a fight with a bullwhacker full of fire and smoke after a long trip.

The bullwhacker had finished up, splendidly unconscious, in a heap of broken bottles at the back of Muldooney's Bar. The owner had decided that the young McLowry lacked the temperament suited to the task of slinging beer and whisky.

Next, McLowry had spent five years in the service of the Texas Rangers. And now, here he was, a drifter, one might say; certainly a man on the prod, imbued with a poison that was labelled revenge, hunting for someone who bore a Boothill brand.

There were faces shrouded in those hazy naphtha flares as well, some smooth-shaven and lighthearted, some bristling with whiskers, and ugly as any hell's brew. There were soft red lips also, seductive voices, and even more seductive curves.

McLowry laughed suddenly, with harshness, consigning the ghosts to the shades from whence they had come.

At a street crossing a crazy cat flew out of an alley, spitting and growling as good as any dog. Then another cat charged past and leaped at the first one. They rolled and screamed and tore at each other, and McLowry hurried away from the display of terrible savagery.

The town buildings tailed off eventually to the railroad station with its mellow-eyed station house. Here were shipping pens, and chutes that were still redolent of sweat and manure and sheer animal presence.

He halted and filled his lungs with the air. It really was a clean smell, free of smoke and grime, slightly spiced with the scent of grass and sage and piney woods. Or was that simply his imagination hitting fever pitch again?

He betrayed a quick start when a figure came out of the shadows.

"Got a match, mister?"

There was a big hat that shielded the

face, but McLowry had an impression of wide shoulders and sharp eyes. Tension rippled along his nerves like a whip being snapped in the air.

"Reckon so." He produced his tin matchbox with his left hand and watched the man poke a cigarette between his lips.

"Hope I ain't troubling you . . . "

"Least trouble I ever had."

The man fingered out a match and struck it, and McLowry's eyes puckered. He saw gaunt jaws that sloped off into shadow. Pools of that same shadow blackened the section of the face immediately below the eyes, so that the whole represented a grotesque mask. There was a vague smell of sweat in the nearness, of horses and leather. The cigarette brought to a red point, the man held the match out of his cupped hands so that the flare hit McLowry's features in brief illumination. The light died, thickening the darkness.

"Name of McLowry?"

The warning came a split second

before the blow from behind. He was swinging to meet the rustle of sound at his back when something exploded at the base of his neck and dropped him to his knees.

He clawed at the dirt, fighting against the sense-throttling pain and dizziness. He had a sensation of being dragged upwards, of hanging suspended in mid-air. Then another wicked blow, this time on the side of his head, and he was in the dirt once more, lights bursting crazily in his brain.

A voice reached him through the confusion.

"This is nothing compared with what you'll get later. Hear me, bucko? A six-by-three Boothill bunk with nobody to disturb your sleep. Get it?"

A boot in the ribs emphasised the warning, and after that McLowry was left alone to consider the multitude of firecrackers going off in his brain. The Chinese crackers sputtered and hissed and stung his eyes. He wanted to move to a safer vantage point, but he was held fast in the agony. He had no idea of how long the torture continued, but there came a time when the firecrackers stopped and all he had to do was discover what they had done with the brain itself.

He was semi-conscious when someone tried separating an arm from his body. He steeled himself against the kick that never came. Instead, a soft voice broke through the layers of frustation and pain.

"Señor McLowry . . . Are you all right?"

Scuffling feet receded and went away. Hooves threshed past and hard laughter rang like the clashing of cracked church bells.

"Damn drunk . . . Near rode over him. Hey, you'd better crawl out of the road, friend, else you're going to get your skull busted up."

Silence and pain and darkness.

There were other sounds presently. The clip-clop of small, chopping hooves.

Then a hand touched his shoulder, tugged gently.

"Can you stand up, *amigo*? I have brought the mule."

He was barely conscious of Pedro Juarez loading him on to the beast. The short journey to the Mexican's hut at the edge of Broken Horn seemed endless. It was dawn before Frank McLowry was able to put any sort of reliance on his senses.

Pedro was preparing coffee and tortillas on a small stove in the middle of the dirt floor. He had given Frank his bed in one end of the room. The Mexican watched curiously as he sat up and rubbed his head and the back of his neck.

"How are you, señor?"

"*Malo*, Pedro. Real bad. You're seeing what looks like a full-grown man with the wit of a month-old babe. I fell for one of the easiest tricks there are."

"I'm afraid I do not understand, señor."

19

"This gent came to me in the dark. Asked for a match. Then boom! On the back of my head."

"There was more than one?"

"Two at least." He took a mug of the steaming coffee. Pedro offered a platter of tortillas.

"Can you eat?"

"Guess so, pard. Unless that gent left some of his boot leather in my stomach."

Pedro sat on a stool and studied him while he ate. He smoked pungent-smelling cigarettes made from Mexican tobacco. He cocked his head to one side.

"Someone does not want you in town? Remember the other one."

"Emmet? Yes, I know. Somebody has made it plenty plain that I ought to get out while I can crawl, never mind walk, and *muy pronto!*"

"But you will stay?"

The house was growing warmer by the minute. A ribbon of sunlight showed beyond the sack curtain on the window. Several hens clucked and pecked round the doorway. A magnificent red-combed cock made a bold invasion, but left again with measured, dignified slowness when Pedro flapped his hat brim.

"What would you do if you were in my place?"

"I am an old man, señor. But if I were young and strong like you . . . "

"Sure. I thought I had you figured for an old revolutionary warhorse! And I'm staying all right. Maybe I opened my mouth too wide yesterday, and too early in the day. But I thought I might as well find out right off how I stood in Broken Horn. I found out without a doubt! I've a lump on my head, busted ribs, and a stiff neck to prove it."

"They could have killed you."

"That's the funny thing, Pedro. Why didn't they finish the job?"

"Perhaps they wished to warn you first. Perhaps they are afraid of the law."

"Maybe. But that didn't stop them killing Emmet."

Pedro shrugged, lit another cigarette from the stub that was sucked empty. "It is hard to understand."

McLowry was on his second mug of coffee when they heard a horse draw in at the front of the house. He placed the mug to one side and slid his long-barrelled Colt from its holster.

"Early visitor," he commented with dry humour. "You don't have a lady friend comes in the mornings, pard?"

Pedro didn't bother to answer. He was sweating a little, glancing from his guest to the closed door.

"Maybe the pair who tackled me have figured out some other place they'd like to kick."

"I can keep the door closed. I can say I am here alone."

"I don't want you to make a liar out of yourself for me, old son. Just let a little air through the door. I'll take it from there."

The Mexican reached for an old

carbine standing in the corner, then changed his mind and stood waiting until the door rattled under a thundering fist.

"Open up there!"

Pedro shifted to a small side window and drew the sacking to one side in order to peer through. McLowry tried to see out, but all he could discern were a few trees that had patches of white mist trailing about their boles.

The door was hammered once more; this time the thumping was really fierce and prolonged. Pedro dropped the curtain and faced McLowry. He was tight-faced with concern, but there was no sign of what could be called outright fear.

"A man with a horse. Another horse without a man."

"It's all right, pard. Let them in." McLowry eased the hammer of his gun back as he spoke. The click he made was solid and reassuring. He wondered if he would have to shoot someone.

He wondered if he was ready to shoot someone.

Pedro opened the door to reveal a lanky, stoop-shouldered man. There was morning dew-moisture on his brows and lashes, and the brim of his hat was embellished with little glistening beads that began to drip. Beyond him Frank could see a thick-bodied horseman framed in the opening. The light was still poor. Damp, chill air had rushed in with the visitor. The chickens clucked and tried to get in. Pedro booted them out.

McLowry levelled his six-shooter. "Who is it, pard?"

"Señor Bennet and Deakin," the Mexican revealed on the instant McLowry recognised Dan Bennet himself.

"Let them in, Pedro," McLowry grunted in relief. He let the hammer of the Colt down and pushed the weapon out of sight.

2

DEPUTY Jed Deakin poked his head into the room. "Who've you got here?" he demanded. His voice was grouchy, touched with the chill of the morning.

"I guess they're looking for me, Pedro," McLowry said. He came off the bed, fighting a momentary dizziness, and pushed his feet into the boots which the Mexican had left handy.

"He's here all right, Dan," Deakin called over his shoulder.

McLowry watched Sheriff Bennet lever his bulky form to the ground. He draped the reins over his mount's face, and then the deputy stood aside to let him duck through the low door arch.

"Stay out there, Jed."

Deakin shrugged and retreated to the horses. The sheriff came on in and heeled the door shut. He glanced at McLowry, cuffed his hat up a trifle, and went to stand by the stove. He stood there with his buttocks to the heat while Pedro poured a mug of coffee. He grunted thanks and took a drink, smacking his lips appreciatively.

"Thought I'd find you here, mister."

"You've been looking for me?" McLowry queried warily. He fished for his tobacco and began to fashion a cigarette. He regarded the lawman with an expression on his face that was neither belligerent nor submissive.

"Not especially. But the hotel clerk wondered why you didn't turn up last night after booking a room. Then I found your horse at the livery and your gear in the office. Then I thought of Juarez here — "

"You're a smart man, Sheriff," McLowry complimented. He finished twisting the tobacco cylinder and put a match to it.

"That's saying you can tell a stupid man from a smart man," Dan Bennet observed. "Well, maybe you can. But some folks would argue the point you're making about me." He indicated with the steaming mug. "Got in a fight, eh?"

"I was jumped last night. Roughed up some. Pedro came along and helped me."

"So I notice. Juarez appears to have cottoned on to you. A real Johnny-on-the-spot. Ain't that so, Pedro?"

"If you say so, Señor Bennet. You will take more coffee?"

"Thanks, not now. Well, I guess it's time to move along. You can move, Mr McLowry?"

McLowry caught his breath, eyes narrowing. "I suppose I could if I had to. But it's early in the day."

"Not that early," was the brusque rejoinder. "Get the rest of your duds, friend."

"Now hold on, Sheriff," McLowry objected. "It seems to me that I've a right to come and go as I please. To stay right where I am if I want to."

Bennet made a sighing sound and drew his gun. He held it loosely at his side. A smile touched his mouth briefly, then the mouth firmed. "Get your things, like I said. You were in a fight inside the town limits last night. Council's hell on keeping ordinances. Got to bring you back."

"To throw me into jail?"

"Never mentioned jail, did I? Seems to me you've got a mighty strong imagination, Mr McLowry. Let's go."

"But, señor," the Mexican protested. "He is ill, and — "

"Shut up, Pedro," the other growled. "But maybe you want to keep your *amigo* company?"

"Take it easy," McLowry advised the Mexican. "There's more to this than meets the eye, isn't there, Sheriff? And I bet it hasn't to do with fighting inside the town limits. I didn't see the men who jumped me."

"Too bad. But it makes no difference."

"It's because of Emmet, isn't it?" McLowry said in a tight voice. "Maybe

28

you know something about his killing that you don't want to tell me?"

"Jed!" Bennet called, and waited until the deputy had bustled inside, revolver at the ready.

"What's wrong, Dan?"

"Nothing wrong. Just take Mr McLowry out of here. We're going to escort him to the livery."

The sheriff left the house first and Jed Deakin jerked his head, twitching his gun at the same time. "After you, mister."

McLowry looked at the Mexican. "Thanks for everything, Pedro. I'll see you around."

"It was a pleasure, señor." Juarez took Frank's outstretched hand, and at the same time his lips fluttered in almost soundless motion. McLowry caught 'Anvil Mesa', and hesitated. But the Mexican dipped his head and stepped back to let the two men leave.

McLowry was escorted through the grey light by the two lawmen. They reached the livery stable and went inside. Dan Bennet headed off to the small office and stirred the sleeping hostler.

"Get this gent his horse," he told the stableman. "And his gear."

Soon McLowry's saddle and accoutrements were handed over. He stood scratching his head while McLowry saddled up and then poked for money to pay. Dan Bennet ushered him out to the street and signalled for the big man to mount.

"What's the big idea, Sheriff? I don't feel too good. I need a proper breakfast."

"You look good enough to me," was the meagre response. "And you'll get a bite somewhere along the trail."

"The trail?"

"That's what it's called. Now, here's what it adds up to, friend: you can promise me to start riding and keep going, or Jed here can herd you a few miles and make sure you keep going."

"Don't give me a lot of choice, do

you?" McLowry said bitterly. "Know what, Sheriff? It strikes me that you're mighty scared of something."

"Not of you, mister," was the heated reply. "Now get."

"No, not of me," McLowry agreed. "But I'd like to know who. The birds who worked me over? They were scared, too. They wouldn't have done what they did if they hadn't been scared."

"So everybody's scared of something," Bennet sneered. "So what were these birds scared of?"

"Can't be dead certain, but I can make a sure as hell guess. They don't want me to find out how Emmet was killed."

"Don't flatter yourself too much, friend. Healthiest thing you can do right now is punch the breeze. And make sure you keep it burning until Broken Horn is just a place you heard of."

"What if I come back?"

Jed Deakin coughed to keep from

smirking at the big fellow's exhibition of cold nerve. Dan Bennet flung him a bleak look and aimed a forefinger at the man on the black horse.

"Are you fool enough to spurn the best advice you'll ever get?"

"Could be I am, sir."

"Then there's only one thing I've got to say to you, McLowry, it'll be *your* funeral."

The pair stood back, making it plain that any further argument would prove useless. McLowry glimpsed the grey shape of the stableman framed in the gateway.

"How do I get to Anvil Mesa?" he queried blandly.

He might as well have dropped a stick of dynamite at the feet of the star-packers. The deputy seemed to be the more frightened of the two. He swore softly, and Dan Bennet looked as if he might drag his gun out and start shooting.

"What do you want at Anvil Mesa?" the sheriff got out at length.

McLowry straightened his hat carefully, fingered his bruised ribs. He wished Pedro Juarez had explained about Anvil Mesa when he had the opportunity and there was no one around to hear what they said. "Maybe I'm just curious about the name," he suggested. "Thing is, how do I get there?"

"I wouldn't advise you — "

"I don't want you to," McLowry bit in on the sentence. His manner was impatient now. He regarded the two men coldly. "What's wrong with a straight answer? Or is all of this range so damn scared that a man isn't safe riding anywhere?"

Dan Bennet had his revolver out before he finished speaking. All he did was gesture with it, the message being that the newcomer to Broken Horn could cut his losses and drift, or stay where he was and risk a bullet. The frightened stableman was there to swear later that the upstart McLowry had gone for his gun first.

McLowry inclined his head in a parting salute, bestowed a wintry smile on the pair, and gigged his horse out into the roadway. They watched him halt at a store that was just opening, frowned worriedly when he dismounted and hitched the black before going inside. They remained where they were, grim and silent, until the tall man emerged with several objects cradled in his arms. These he stored in his saddlebags before mounting and riding on out of town.

When he could no longer see Frank McLowry, nor hear the measured hoofbeats of that big black horse, Dan Bennet released a breath he appeared to have been holding for the past ten minutes.

"I hope to heck that's the last we'll see of him."

Deakin's eyes held a secret glint. "But you don't figure it is?"

"Hell no, I don't figure it is, Jed. I've got a bad feeling about that one. He could cause more trouble than a reservation bust-out."

"Maybe I should follow him for a spell!"

"Be a waste of time. But say . . . where did he get hold of that Anvil Mesa stuff? Did Juarez?"

"Maybe so. Still, he didn't know the way, and Juarez could have told him."

★ ★ ★

Frank McLowry skirted the squat, unlovely upheaval of timber, red adobe and brick that was the northern fringe of Broken Horn and eyed the rails twisting away into the light of a new day. Soon there would be a blazing sun in the sky and that breathless heat would assert itself. Once more kids would come to listen to the humming of the rails and to dream of the wonderful worlds to be explored at rail-ends. As it was, just then the shipping pens were empty and they stank just as always. A thin cord curl of blue-grey smoke was coming from the station house chimney as McLowry pressed his black towards it.

A lean, moustached man watched his approach from a small window, and he was at the open door by the time McLowry reined in. It was obvious from the way his mouth changed that he had taken the visitor for someone else.

"Hello," he greeted. "Thought at first you were Marve Collins. Couldn't think why you were so early." He laughed. "Train doesn't get in until ten at the earliest." He drew a nervous breath; "You're new to these parts, aren't you? But wait a minute . . . Haven't I seen you somewhere before?"

McLowry grinned at him. "Looks like you figure you've seen a ghost come out of the graveyard to haunt the whole damn town. Know something," he went on easily, "this is one burg could sure do with a good haunting."

"Amen to that!" the other agreed with a sudden burst of laughter. "Yes, you could be a ghost right enough. And I might know what you're talking about. But you're a bit taller than he was. And, if you'll forgive me saying so, you haven't got the same go-to-blazes look in your eyes. You're more careful, maybe. Or are you . . . ? Careful men don't get into fights that leave blue welts and bruises."

"You knew my brother, didn't you, Mr — "

"Grober. Sam Grober." The initial willingness to exchange talk and banter appeared to vanish and the station agent suddenly looked diffident and strained. "But if you ask me anything else . . . "

McLowry was out of his saddle by then and touching his ribs with a gloved hand. "I think I understand," he said wryly. "I bet there's a whole lot more you could say, and maybe would like to say. But you're scared, I guess? Well, never mind. I'll find out what I want to know one way or another. Would it hurt much to give me the direction to Anvil Mesa?"

It was impossible to say whether the mesa meant anything to Grober. He looked away beyond his visitor to the fringes of the town while his face reddened. He pulled himself together and indicated he had business in his office. "You're headed in the wrong direction anyhow," he allowed. "Better go on round the town and pick up the stage road that links with Gopher Flats. Three or four miles out you switch to the south."

"Thanks a heap, Mr Grober."

Grober attempted to regain his earlier confident manner. He essayed a weak smile. "You know, you really do look a bit like Marve Collins, too."

"That so? Thanks a heap, sir. Oh, by the way, who is this Marve Collins anyhow?"

"Rancher from White River way."

"Thanks again."

"Welcome!"

'*Hope you don't sicken with fright and throw up, mister . . .* '

38

McLowry regarded the outskirts of the town with hooded, wary eyes as he circled it. On the way he made the acquaintance of several touchy mongrels that seemed to share the prevailing opinion of him. One of them followed him until he reached the stage road that twined like a faded ragged ribbon over hills and hollows into the southwest. Here, he looked across his shoulder and spotted a mounted figure in the middle distance. Sheriff Dan Bennet, without doubt.

He wondered if Bennet intended to stick to his trail, but after a while, when he saw that the sweep of land behind him was innocently empty, he surmised that all the lawman had wished to do was make sure the unwelcome visitor was moving out.

Soon the saddle-rocking managed to bring McLowry's aches and bruises back to life. He continued to ride steadily, unhurriedly and alertly, scanning the rocks and stands of trees that bordered the stage road for a couple of miles. He reflected on the effect of his mention of Anvil Mesa on the lawmen and the station agent. He might as well have been asking the way to Hades for the reaction he had received. He wished that Pedro Juarez had told him more, that he had called with Juarez before leaving so that he might hear the whole story. And thinking of the Mexican himself, McLowry wondered if he was all he appeared to be. What would he find at Anvil Mesa anyhow — a clue to the killing of his brother? And if the place could not furnish some of the information he needed, why had Juarez directed him there?

At the end of another half-hour McLowry knew that someone really was dogging his tracks.

He continued for another ten minutes, then drew the black up and dismounted, pretending to examine a hind hoof. He glanced behind him, but due to the road winding over a series of undulations, it was impossible to see anyone.

He eyed the way ahead, followed the course of the stage road until it bent around the shoulder of a mountain. He pushed his horse into a fast lope until he gained a point where his back-trail was hidden, and where he would be visible to his trailer only when that worthy rounded the grey outcropping of rock.

To make the surprise complete, he guided the black off the road and into a thicket of jack-pine thicket, then slid from the saddle. He unlimbered his Colt and settled down to wait at the base of a weathered boulder.

At first he fancied the rider had halted. There was nothing to be heard in all that silent wilderness. Then he picked up the drumming of hooves. It was as if the man now feared he might get too far away from him.

A hard smile deepened the wrinkles at the corners of McLowry's eyes, accentuated the twin grooves running out from his mouth like knife tracks. Sheriff Dan Bennet again, he wondered. The deputy, Jed Deakin? One of the men who had jumped him last night? His senses tingled with anticipation.

His trained ear had told him that only one horse was travelling on the road, and this fact was puzzling in itself. The rider might well be a stranger, bent on some business of his own. But better to make doubly sure than to risk catching a bullet in the back.

He tensed when the horseman drew closer. He was almost at the rock shoulder, and continuing to ride pretty fast. McLowry raised his head slightly when a dun form wheeled into view. Then he saw the rider, poised lightly in his saddle. From this distance it was impossible to say whether the man was known to him.

He ducked as the horse drew level with the thicket, was dragged to a rough halt. He knew the moment when the other dismounted, and anger began to churn in him. He was certain now that this was neither the sheriff nor his deputy. One of the toughs who had beaten him up?

At the scuffle of boots on the hard ground he peered through the cluster of jack-pine. The newcomer was thin enough, not too tall, clad in checkered shirt and wide-brimmed sombrero. He appeared to be scanning the roadside, wanting to see if his quarry had angled out here. The black whickered suddenly and McLowry swore.

There was nothing else for it but to step quickly into the open, gun levelled on the stranger. He found himself pinned by a fearful stare.

"All right, mister," McLowry breathed. "Hold it right there."

For a spine-chilling instant he was sure the other would make a try for the gun dangling at his hip. The fingers of the gloved right hand opened, dropped, and froze, all in the space of a couple of seconds. Then both hands moved slowly aloft.

"That's showing a grain of sense."

McLowry took a few steps closer to the other, careful to avoid roots and rock snags. "Now maybe you'll tell me who you are and why the devil you've been following me."

"But I — I haven't been following you . . ."

"Don't lie, kid," McLowry snapped. He had seen wet-behind-ears youngsters who would cut a man's throat for a dollar. "It's plain to see you're only a button and this trailing game is new to you. Talk now, and make it fast."

The only reaction was a widening of the eyes and a parting of the lips, and McLowry wondered if this wasn't more from surprise than fear. The silence brought his anger to boiling point. One thing he was sure of, however, the man before him was not one of the attackers of last night. He was much too slender, for a start, and he had no signs of the rough-house specialist.

"Are you going to start talking or do I have to plant a slug in your mangy hide?"

"I — I told you I wasn't following you," was the heated rejoinder.

"Liar!"

In his rising fury he took a few more steps that put him directly in front of the man. His left hand flicked out and rocked the head back. The youngster stumbled under the blow and fell. He dropped his head so that the hat brim hid his face. The narrow shoulders began to shake.

McLowry swallowed thickly. Revulsion rose in him. "You're man enough to fork a horse out on my trail," he raged. "But when it comes to meeting someone face to face it's a different matter, isn't it?"

He reached down and caught the slim shoulder, amazed at the softness of the flesh beneath his fingers. For some odd reason he knew a pang of remorse.

"All right, kid. Quit snivelling and get to your feet. I won't be too rough with you if you spill the beans. But no bluffing."

"What — what are you talking about?"

The head was lifted back and the moist purple eyes that shone on him were wide and stricken, at the same time strangely triumphant. It was as if the youngster had some secret knowledge, wielded some power that might be utilised at any moment. McLowry caught his breath, studied the features more closely. The face was fine, delicately chiselled, even for a youth. What would his age be — sixteen, seventeen? Certainly no more. There was a dusting of freckles over the bridge of the short, slightly uptilted nose. The mouth was far too red, too soft. A long lock of straw-yellow hair fell from the confines of the hat and lay like a wisp of gold across the high, narrow forehead.

McLowry was almost beyond reasoning now. The whole business was taking on the flavour of a bad nightmare. Nevertheless, his eyes persisted in running over the slim body; they

46

marvelled at the full roundness of a woman's bosom. And then he fell back as if a mighty hand had been sent crashing into his face.

"Hell!" he breathed.

"I told you," she whispered huskily.

"Why — why didn't you tell me right off?" he choked. "Why did you play games with me? Why did you let me hit you like that?" He was groaning now, mumbling unintelligibly.

Scorn lighted the purple eyes for an instant. It passed, and then a flicker of amusement lent a different radiance. She sensed the way power and dominance had been transferred. She rose to her feet, and when McLowry managed to get his limbs to function and extended a hand to help her, she shook him off.

"I can manage, thank you, unless you wish to knock me down again."

"Look, I'm sorry if I — "

"Forget it. I lost a bracelet around here a week ago. I thought I would come and search for it."

He studied her for a while, casting his mind back, recalling the shadow on the trail, the hoofbeats, the quickening of pace. He licked dry lips.

"Let me help you."

"There's no need to. I expect it's like searching for a needle in a haystack. It's just that it had particular sentimental value. I must have searched a dozen times already." She dusted herself off, settled her hat, and pushed the strands of gold away out of sight. She was going to her horse when he found his tongue again.

"Is there anything I can to to make amends?"

"Not really. It probably was my fault as much as yours. Mr — "

"McLowry," he supplied quickly. He waited for some sort of reaction and was disappointed when none was forthcoming.

She toed into the stirrup and lifted herself lightly to the saddle of the dun horse. "I'd better be off."

"Ma'am, I'll be pleased to escort you

to wherever you're headed."

"Thank you again, Mr McLowry. But I think I'll be able to finish my journey. I'm sure I won't encounter any more . . . obstacles."

His face burned as he watched her turn out to the road and touch the dun's flanks with her heels. She kept going steadily, not looking back, and when at last she topped out a rise and went from his view, he had the feeling that the toughs had really unsettled his wits last night and that this hallucination was the result.

3

IT was some minutes before McLowry could assemble his thoughts to the extent of making a clear review of the incident which he now saw as a sinister plot into which he had been inadvertently dragged. It was he who was the innocent victim, whatever the girl believed, he tried telling himself.

At length he swore heartily and brought his black horse out of the jack-pine thicket.

Of course she had tricked him, manoeuvred him into a position where he had been obliged to apologise needlessly. By this time she was likely laughing her head off, congratulating herself on the way she had fooled him and consequently slipped through his fingers.

"Was she trailing me after all . . . "

Aboard Blackie, and riding on around

the loop in the road, he fell to wondering who she really was. That she had looks went without saying. Even that cowboy get-up could do nothing to detract from her sheer femininity. But all that talk about a missing bracelet was just so much hogwash dreamed up on the spur of the moment.

He was soon able to see her in the distance. She was still riding hard and bearing into the south, away from the white ribbon of road. He was tempted to hurry after her, demand an explanation. But he realised that he would look foolish and, in any case, it was unlikely he would learn more about her than she was willing to tell.

When he arrived at the point where the girl had swung out from the road he saw a beaten track, not wide, but pretty well used all the same. He thought about the station agent's directions and turned on to the track. There was a screen of trees ahead and the girl had vanished beyond this. Another possibility arose — was she making for the location known as Anvil Mesa?

On the other side of the timber the land became harsh and raw in the extreme. Long ridges of rock spread out in fan-shaped array. On McLowry's left, a tumble of hills banked up to a beetling cliff wall that was five or six miles in length and thinned away into the shimmering stillness. On his right, the land fell off in broken billow and roll, grey and green and brown, and this likewise faded into the haze of far distance.

The sun was climbing out of the east like a beast uncaged. It looked fiery and red, and would soon remind the world who the real boss was. But just then it was indulging itself, performing like a skilful artist. It painted cliff and butte and turret, soon transforming a forbidding wilderness into a wonderland of colour. Far out and down a gradual slope, McLowry spotted the flight of the girl. She rode a dim trail that twisted off into more timber. She reached the timber and that trail, too, was swallowed in the sun-splashed woodland.

McLowry pressed on, not hurrying the black, content to stay in the wake of the girl. He had a growing conviction that down there he would find the place known as Anvil Mesa. It just had to be a mesa shaped like a smithy's anvil. But what else he might find was as big a mystery as the girl herself and this awesome, complex land.

A half-hour later he was well into the timber and still following an easily recognizable trail that wound through matted aisles and came out on a broad sweep of grassland.

He hauled the black in to purse his lips and stare. The grass rolled off in all directions. Far out he glimpsed cattle. There was no trace of the girl now. He fashioned a cigarette and pushed Blackie across a meadow. They dropped down to a creek that cut an irregular course from due east to due west. He let the horse blow and have a drink.

Suddenly he saw the mesa. It was over on his left, dark and gloomy around its massive base, but flushed with pink half-way up, and burning with red fire where its flat top caught the full force of the sunlight.

"Anvil Mesa, sure as little apples!"

Curiosity consumed him now and he nudged his horse on over the grass, passing bunches of cattle, rousing rabbits and grouse. A bull-snake popped its head out of a gopher hole and he drew Blackie aside. He hit another trail that widened and led him to the curving banks of a river. He had no trouble fording it and reached the opposite shore in a dark cloud of heel-flies.

Now he was moving along a cottonwood-lined avenue that was cool and shadowy. The mesa hovered out there on his left, a huge bastion against the northern wilderness and perhaps the snow and hail that would lash across in winter. The avenue took a sudden S-shaped twist and he saw a wide gateway and, beyond, numerous outhouses, then a stone and timber ranch-house poised on a shelf of granite.

Steps led from the yard to the high porch. The porch was railed and commanded a fine view of the avenue approach. McLowry glimpsed a man sitting on a bench, a big man in open-necked shirt and hat balanced on the crown of his head. He watched the newcomer swing through the gateway and bring his horse to a standstill. Then he hefted the rifle that had lain across his thighs and aimed it at McLowry's chest.

"Hold on."

McLowry forced a wry grin. This was the location Pedro Juarez had been indicating when he whispered Anvil Mesa; of that he was sure. But Sheriff Dan Bennet and his deputy had appeared to almost recoil at mention of the name. Which meant there could be danger lurking in this rangeland paradise.

"I'm Frank McLowry," he began to explain to the man on the porch. "I thought if I headed out here I might find . . . " He broke off, moistening his lips.

The man with the rifle continued to stare at him in a dispassionate fashion, saying nothing, letting the stranger drown himself in his own confusion. The rifle remained trained on his chest, fanning a slow anger. McLowry burst out recklessly, "Where's the girl I trailed here?"

"You started to say something," the other reminded him, speaking in a slow drawl. "Why didn't you finish it? You came here to find what?"

"That girl."

"You're a liar. State your reason for riding in here. You came from Broken Horn way?"

McLowry felt his heart lurching in his breast. He cuffed his hat up and started to slide out of the saddle.

The voice cracked at him, carrying a whiplash threat.

"Stay where you are until you're invited to light. Now talk, or else get the devil out of here."

"All right, I'll talk." McLowry steeled himself. "Did you know Emmet McLowry?"

"You're hell on asking questions, ain't you?" the other droned impatiently. "Talk or git!"

McLowry was forced to remain in his saddle. He leaned over the pommel with both hands well in the man's view. "I hit Broken Horn because I got a hint my brother finished up there. It was the end of a lot of travelling, of asking straight questions that usually got crooked answers. It took me an hour in town to find out where Emmet was buried. Then, last night, I was tackled by a couple of toughs. A Mexican brought me home and patched me up. This morning the sheriff dropped by and told me to drift."

"So you drifted?" There was faint contempt in the slow drawl.

"For the time being anyhow. A man can't operate too well from an iron cage. And I certainly intend to operate, mister."

"You sound like you're planning to be a pretty big wheel. So now we're at the place where the sheriff gave you the tramp's rush . . . "

"That's right. I got a tip to head for Anvil Mesa. But don't ask me why, because I don't know myself. Along the trail I — "

"Who told you to come here?" the inquisitor demanded. "The law?"

"No. Look . . . it doesn't matter."

"Suit yourself. So you're at Anvil spread, and you want to do some more chin-wagging?"

"A girl followed me. At least I thought she was following me. I took her for a man, and I guess I was a bit rough with her. I figured I was being set up for another hammering by the toughs who — "

TBB2

"All right, forget the rest," the man interrupted once more. "Come on up here till I get a better gander at you."

McLowry frowned. He felt sore, angry and humiliated. He hesitated, wondering what new danger he was about to walk into. Apart from this big man on the porch bench, the area around the ranch-house seemed deserted. He was tempted to spur the black through the wide gateway and take a chance on being shot at. The dark bore of the rifle pushed the thought away. Getting himself killed would solve nothing.

He dropped from the saddle and headed for the porch steps. The rifle barrel moved along with him, as if his body attracted it like a magnet. He reached the porch and halted. The man remained seated and McLowry had an opportunity to study his features. They were craggy and solid, square in the jawline, aggressive in the set of the chin. The man was about fifty. The eyes that ran over the visitor were a faded blue, and resembled in some fashion the much-scrubbed blue shirt. The body itself was thick and well packed with muscle. McLowry found himself wondering why he continued to sit.

He forced a grin, made a little gesture with his hands. "Well, you can see me."

"Yeah, I can see you."

"So what happens now? Do you shoot me straight off or do you want to take time to think about it?"

If he imagined this would strike a different sort of spark he was disappointed. The indifferent appraisal went on for another half-minute, and McLowry tried guessing at the thoughts running behind the shaggy brow. The stillness of the place and the manner of the man on the bench began rasping at his nerves.

"Can I go now?" he asked testily. "Something tells me I'm in the wrong place after all."

He had his foot on the top step

when the man barked: "Stay where you are."

"You can't stop me if I want to go."

"Maybe I can't. Maybe I could if I took it into my head. Let it simmer for a minute . . . Hey, Jenny!"

McLowry jerked at the shout, saw the girl emerge from the front door of the house. It was the same girl he believed had followed him out of Broken Horn. She was somewhat pale now, but her mouth — so much like the man's in many ways — was set in a firm line.

"Is this the one, Jenny?"

The girl nodded, evading the visitor's curious gaze. "Yes, it's him. It's impossible to be mistaken."

"Sure about that? Sure he's a McLowry and not some upstart that looks like Emmet?"

"How — how can I be absolutely sure, Dad?"

"Try and make up your mind."

The purple eyes lifted to McLowry's,

held for an instant while colour crept slowly into the smooth cheeks. She nodded again. "I believe he is who he said he is. He was beaten up last night, and . . . Well, I know that he's been making a lot of inquiries."

"So he really must be Frank?"

"He must be, Dad."

McLowry cuffed a layer of sweat from his brow. He had the sensation of being the central character in a farce. But no, that was not quite true. The situation was serious enough and warranted all the patience and understanding he could bring to bear. Still, he couldn't help letting a certain irony tinge his voice.

"Well, if everybody has had their say, and if everybody is agreed on that point, maybe you'd like me to prove it," he suggested. "Like me to tell you that my brother and I were raised in Indiana, that Emmet went to school for about a year in his life, that he was mad on shooting and fishing and riding frisky horses? He had a mole on the left side of his face and a knife scar on his right ribs where he was stabbed by a crazy character who was making trouble for a woman? And if you want to know why I'm in this neck of the woods, it's because I — "

"That's enough!"

The man on the bench laid his rifle aside and tried to get to his feet. The girl hurried to him, gripped his arm, and told him to take it easy. McLowry stared while she let him sink down again.

"Are you — hurt, Mister?"

"A little," was the meagre response. "But I'll mend. Bullet went clear across my spine. Thought at first I was done for. But the doc gave me a chance. Only . . . it's pure hell not being able to get around."

"You'll just have to be patient, Dad," the girl chided. "Otherwise you'll undo everything."

"Sure, honey. I know, I told you I'd take it easy, didn't I? Did you ever see anybody taking it so dadblamed easy?" A wry grin broke through the frustration. "Sorry I acted tough with you, Mr McLowry. But the way things are at the minute, it's the only way to get along."

McLowry frowned and was about to ask the obvious question. He chewed it back, said instead: "It's certainly a fine spread you've got here. It's the kind of place a man dreams about nights. But where are your riders?"

The other emitted a harsh laugh. "Riders? Well, we used to have a crew. A good crew, when I come to think of it. But I guess nobody could blame the boys for lighting out when Split C decided to take over this country and everything standing on it."

"Split C?"

"You've never heard of it?"

"Dad, how could he?" the girl said with a trace of weariness in her tone. "If Mr McLowry's new to this country he can't know what's going on. He likely doesn't even know who we are."

"You're right, ma'am." Now that

there was no rifle covering him, he relaxed somewhat. Yet a tension still clawed at him. There was an air of mystery about this ranch, even tragedy. And he knew that, somehow, his brother had been mixed up in it. "My name's Frank," he added.

"Sorry, Frank," the girl's father apologised. "You've already met my daughter. She told me how you took her for a man and tackled her. But I guess it serves her right for gadding about like a tomboy. Anyhow, you've gathered that her name's Jenny, after her mother who has been dead these three years. Name's Sanderson, Clem Sanderson. This is Anvil ranch, so called for that mesa." As he spoke, Sanderson extended his hand and McLowry shook it.

He felt that he might be getting somewhere at last.

Sanderson invited him into the house, and McLowry and the girl helped him along a short hallway and into a tastefully furnished parlour where he sank into an easy chair. The chair stood beneath the window overlooking the front yard, and the girl placed his rifle beside him where he could reach it easily. McLowry could well imagine Clem Sanderson placing that weapon by the side of his bed at night before he went to sleep.

The girl regarded the visitor with some diffidence, yet the smile that crossed her face retained a trace of her hell-raising spirit.

"I'm sorry if I fooled you back on the trail, Mr McLowry. But the way things are — "

"You don't have to explain," he interrupted. "And the name's Frank, remember."

"Of course. Then we can call it quits?"

"I'll be real happy to do that, Jenny."

"You can put your horse out in the corral," Sanderson suggested. "You can get grain and whatever else you need in the barn. And I hope I don't have to ask you more than once to make yourself at home."

"That's handsome of you, sir."

"I'll start a meal when you've gone," Jenny said. "I'm sure you're hungry."

"Not overly. I had a bite before Sheriff Bennet made me leave town."

At mention of the lawman, a frown darkened the girl's features and she glanced at her father. Neither of them commented, however, and McLowry went on out. He took the black around the end of the house and stripped it at the corral. There were half a dozen saddle horses frisking in the enclosure, not many for a ranch of this size. He turned the black loose and lingered at the fence to roll a cigarette and get it going. He smoked thoughtfully, taking in everything.

The ranch lay-out was beginning to show signs of neglect. The door of the barn hung askew for want of a new hinge. The barn itself was weather-bleached, and he noted a lot of loose shakes. Weeds sprouted thickly around the main building, and the small bunkhouse across the way squatted forlornly. A window was broken and the roof needed fixing.

Questions pushed themselves to the front of McLowry's mind now. What had Split C done to bring about such a state of affairs? What power did Split C wield, and what fear had it instilled in the men who used to work here? Certainly this hadn't been a fighting outfit. The main question of course was; where had his brother Emmet fitted in?

Back in the house, the girl served up steak and potatoes. The food was cooked just the way McLowry liked, and afterwards he fashioned another cigarette while Clem Sanderson produced a pipe and tobacco. The meal had been conducted in an atmosphere of small talk and irrelevancies, and now Mclowry felt the time was ripe.

"Mr Sanderson, I won't beat around things," he began. "You know that I'm here to find out all I can about my brother and the manner of his death.

If you can help me at all I'll be more than grateful."

The rancher finished tamping tobacco into the bowl of his pipe and scratched a match alight. He eyed the tall, craggy-featured man through a cloud of grey smoke.

"Frank, right off I must tell you that I don't know who fired the shots that killed Emmet in the street of Broken Horn. But I'm sure I know who was behind the shooting."

"Dad . . . " The girl touched her father's arm. "You could be wrong, you know. Just because Marve Collins has forced us to the wall, it doesn't mean he was responsible for Emmet's death."

"Marve Collins?" McLowry murmured. "Where have I heard that name? Oh, yes, the station agent. Seems Collins runs a spread somewhere in the White River region."

"That's him, Frank," Sanderson agreed with a weighty nod. "He's a heartless scoundrel. A range buzzard's what I call him. He has brought me to the point of ruin. He had his men bushwhack me. It's a wonder they didn't finish me off when they were at it."

"But, Dad, you can't be absolutely sure that — "

"Wait, honey. This is Emmet's brother, and he's entitled to hear what I know, and what I think about the whole business. I'll tell you what has happened so far, Frank, and you can take it from there."

McLowry listened intently. The story Clem Sanderson had to tell had little to offer by way of originality. The story was as old as the West itself. The Anvil ranch had been a prosperous outfit until three years ago, when Jenny's mother died and Marve Collins had cast his eye on the girl. McLowry swallowed thickly as he listened, and a frown sat on his brow like a thunder cloud.

Jenny had danced with Collins a couple of times in Broken Horn but had attached no significance to the young rancher's overtures. Every cowboy thought he was in love with the daughter of Clem Sanderson. But whereas most of the punchers were courteous and respected her reserve, Marve Collins had forced his case to the point where Jenny had to make it clear that a line must be drawn and that Collins, no matter how rich and powerful he was, must toe that line. In short, Jenny was not prepared to fall into the Split C owner's arms, as he believed she would.

"After that things got worse," Sanderson explained. "Marve rode over here one day and I had to order him off at rifle point. He turned nasty, showed the true side of his nature, I reckon. Anyhow, he threatened me, threatened what he would do to my ranch and my crew."

"What did you do about it?"

"I laughed it off, not that I really felt

it was much of a laughing matter. And as it turned out, things went from bad to worse. My cattle were scattered, so that it took days some times to catch them and bring them back to home range. Then one of my boys was killed, shot in the back. Nobody had seen it happen, nobody could point a finger at Split C. But it was plain as the nose on your face what had happened. Sheriff Dan Bennet made a show of hunting for the killer, but Bennet's under Marve's thumb. Split C can carry plenty of weight in an election, a sight more weight than the likes of me can carry.

"It got worse and worse. Another of my boys was bushwhacked, wounded pretty badly, and that was the last straw. By the end of that month all but one of my riders wanted his time. Then he went, too. But I still held on, Emmet and me, that is."

"Emmet was here with you?" McLowry queried hoarsely.

"He was my ramrod, Frank. Had

been for two years. Ever since the day he rode past the mesa and spotted Jenny. But they got him as well — "

Sanderson broke off, and McLowry heard the girl weeping softly.

4

SO now he had it — the motive behind the killing of Emmet. It might have been cloaked under a veneer of spite and bad feeling directed at the Anvil Mesa ranch; it might even have been contrived so that Clem Sanderson would feel responsible in that he had hired Emmet in the first place. It would have done Marve Collins no good if rumours got around that he had arranged the murder of Emmet McLowry because of a girl. But it appeared to be the truth, all the same, and McLowry saw no reason to question his logic.

Looking at Jenny Sanderson, he could understand how a weak-minded man with the potential for murder might succumb to his instincts. He could understand, too, how his brother could have fallen in love with this girl, and how Jenny might have responded to Emmet's overtures.

He was silent for so long that Sanderson glanced at his daughter. She had regained her composure, but lines of pain were etched into her face. She was watching McLowry intently.

"You mustn't think that Marve Collins was responsible, Frank," she said hesitantly. "I know that everything seems to point to it, but there is no proof. If there was, Sheriff Bennet would have arrested Marve."

McLowry nodded. "Sure, I understand, Jenny. And I'm grateful to your dad for letting me know so much. Otherwise it might have taken weeks, months maybe, to find out so much."

"What will you do now?" Sanderson asked curiously.

"I don't know. I'll have to think about it. What can I do?" he added with a shrug.

"You could ride out and forget it," the rancher told him. "That way you can keep your hide in one piece.

Collins runs a big spread, and he has plenty of gunhawks on his payroll. He cleared the whole eastern end of his range of the nesters that settled there, scared them out and bought their land when it was put to public sale. I know he has the same plans for this end of the country. Anvil has some of the best grass in the territory, and certainly the best water supply."

"I saw that much," McLowry conceded. "And there's still plenty of cattle running loose."

"You bet there is!" Bitterness soured Sanderson's tone. "Plenty of cattle and grass, and nobody to do the work. It's a hell of a note, mister, especially for a man who had to fight every inch of the way to get where he is."

McLowry said gravely: "I know how you feel. But maybe the tide will turn one of these days."

"Not if I sit here on my rump and wait for it to turn. Things don't happen that way. The world passes the man who waits, and you needn't try to tell me anything different."

"I won't," McLowry smiled. He rose and reached for his hat.

"Can I ask where you're headed?" Sanderson queried.

"I recall you telling me I should clear out while the going's good."

"It's sound advice. This place is just about finished. One of these days the buzzards will flock in to pick the bones."

"Why don't you pull out yourself then? You shouldn't have much trouble selling a spread like this."

"Collins has offered to buy it," the rancher snorted. "But I'll see him in hell before I let him have it."

"What about Jenny? Do you aim to go on putting her at risk? And if Collins is the kind of bird you say he is . . . " McLowry let the rest hang, but the quick flush that entered the girl's cheeks and the thunder-cloud that descended on her father's brow, told him they knew what he meant.

"I've asked her to leave me here,"

Sanderson said defensively. "I'll soon be able to get around again."

"Dad, you know that's silly," the girl retorted. "You wouldn't last a week in your present condition."

"I'd say that's talking horse sense, ma'am," McLowry applauded. "And I reckon the old mossy-horn knows it. The only alternative is to . . ."

Again he let his words trickle off, but this time for a different reason. He had caught a low drumming of hoofbeats coming towards the ranch-house. Sanderson swore and grabbed his rifle.

"Get me back out on the porch," he snapped. "Wait, damn you!" he roared as McLowry wheeled towards the front door. "This is my show."

"You'd better do as he says," the girl advised tautly.

"Very well then. But let's make it fast."

They heaved the rancher out of his chair and started him through the doorway to the porch. McLowry could feel the hard coiling of Sanderson's arm and shoulder muscles as he sank down on the ranch where he had been seated earlier.

"All right, mister," he said urgently to McLowry. "Light out of here before they spot you . . . Damn it, man, don't just stare! It might be the crowd that roughed you up. They could have found out where you are."

"You're running away in front of yourself, old-timer," McLowry complained. "I'm not skedaddling anywhere for the time being. Jenny, you go back inside."

The girl hesitated while the hoofbeats pounded closer. Her eyes clung to McLowry. She seemed puzzled, confused.

"Maybe you ought to go when you can," she said in a tight whisper.

"Inside, ma'am," he ordered sternly. "And stay there until this crowd punches the breeze again."

Still she stared, lips parted slightly, a quality in her regard that had the effect on McLowry's nerves that a bolt of lightning might have. Then she turned wordlessly and darted into the house.

McLowry stood beside Sanderson's bench. The rancher had his rifle pointing at the gateway leading into the yard. McLowry had his own fingers on the walnut stock of his .45 when the first of the riders burst out of the avenue in a cloud of dust and swung under the hanging Anvil sign. Three other horsemen appeared in quick succession, and the man leading them pushed out in front, hauling up a few yards from the porch steps. His companions fanned out behind him. All took care to keep their hands in plain view, and the foremost — a rangy, dark-haired man with a weather-reddened face — stared hard at McLowry.

"What do you want here now, Calkin?" Clem Sanderson demanded stridently. His rifle was on a level with the newcomer's midriff and the man called Calkin was uncomfortably aware of the fact.

Calkin pointed a long finger at

McLowry. "Who's this jasper?"

"None of your damned business who he is," Sanderson sang out recklessly. "But maybe you've got a notion who he looks like. Maybe you've met him already," he added with a grim emphasis that was not lost on the Split C man.

"What are you driving at, Clem? You started talking in riddles?" Calkin's beady eyes left off raking McLowry for an instant to glare at the rancher. He looked puzzled now, slightly off balance.

"Ain't driving at anything if you can't see the point," Sanderson retorted. He gestured with the rifle. "If you've got something to say, Deke, spit it out *pronto*, and then take your friends out of here. Happens you're trespassing."

"We won't be for much longer," the rangy man sneered. "It's only a matter of time, Clem."

"Why, you — "

McLowry sensed that Clem Sanderson was about to unleash a shot, and he knocked the rifle barrel aside. He spoke for the first time since the arrival of the Split C men. "Take it easy, Mr Sanderson. Surely you can see they're trying to push you into something. A bullet jamboree, maybe, with them having most of the fun."

"Say, you're a pretty smart fella, ain't you?" Deke Calkin commented with sour amusement.

"Man doesn't have to be all that smart to get your weight, friend," McLowry said quietly.

"Is that a fact! And when I come to think of it, I've got a hunch I've seen you before somewhere."

A muscle in McLowry's jaw jumped warningly and his eyes chilled. "I've got me a hunch that maybe you have at that."

"A brother, huh?" Calkin's laugh was ragged. "Damn it, yes! Emmet McLowry! Now that was a terrible pity . . ."

"It'll be a pity for the gents that murdered him," McLowry said with deceptive gentleness. "Emmet must have been bushwhacked. He was too sharp to let somebody get the drop on him in a fair do."

Deke Calkin writhed under the implication. His right hand began to slide along his thigh to holstered gun. A slight tensing of the body was McLowry's only reaction.

Clem Sanderson butted in. "Don't you touch that iron, Deke," he said crisply. "Else I'll let a streak of daylight through you."

Calkin froze, drew a slow breath. He made a sweeping motion with his left hand. "We spotted a gent hanging around our cattle," he said by way of justifying the visit. "Trailed him thisaways. What you get to say about that, Clem?"

"Just that I think you're a damn liar," Sanderson grated.

"Now, you mind your tongue for a minute, Clem." Calkin leaned over his saddle-horn, dipped his head towards McLowry. "Could have been that gent standing beside you. Maybe we should take him back with us so Marve can ask him a couple of questions."

"That's fine by me," McLowry purred with a savage smile pulling at the corners of his mouth. "Go ahead and take me, boys."

Deke Calkin jerked back in his saddle, glanced at the men ranged behind him. His cunning eyes glittered while he considered the situation. A heavy silence hung over the yard. One of the horses tossed its head and whickered. From the corner of his eyes McLowry saw a pot-bellied man trying to make a sneak draw.

"Go ahead and try it, fella," he said bleakly. "But make sure you say your prayers before you do."

"It's for your own good," Calkin stormed. It went against his grain to let the stranger take the initiative. "If Marve thinks you're clean he won't hold you. I'm warning you, mister, you'd better get wise to who's the real boss in this neck of the woods."

"Collins sounds like he's got this whole range all tied up with a pink ribbon," McLowry observed sarcastically. "But you tell him if he wants to dicker with me he'd better come visiting himself. And tell him I don't take kindly to sidewinder tricks. Can you remember all that, Mr Calkin?"

The man's face crimsoned with suppressed fury. He was obliged to swallow a couple of times before trusting himself to answer. Then: "Damn right, I'll remember, McLowry. But you'd better tuck something under your own hat as well. You're going to finish up the way Emmet did. And if you're thinking of working for this rundown outfit you're crazy. Marve aims to own all this grass pretty soon. Anybody who tries to buck Split C is bucking big trouble."

"You all through with preaching the gospel according to Marve Collins, friend?"

McLowry's six-shooter had sprung to his hand with a speed that made Calkin gasp. The bore of the gun described a slow circle that embraced all four Split C men.

"Now, you see here, buster — "

"Back up," McLowry said flatly. "Get your horses to rattling their hocks or . . . *make your play!*"

Calkin gulped while his red face turned grey. He stabbed an angry look at Clem Sanderson. Sanderson had decided to let Frank McLowry hold the stage; he was smiling gently, like a man who had been listening to something good for a change, something that sounded like music to his ears. His rifle described a lazy circle.

"Deke, if I was in your boots right now I'd pay good heed to what Frank just said."

"You're a damn fool, Clem," Calkin hissed. "You're digging a hole for yourself."

The Split C man who had eased himself out on McLowry's left snatched his gun clear, eared back the hammer, and fired. His horse had reared on the same instant and the bullet went wild, but the danger signal had pulsed home to McLowry's brain and his big .45 spat flame. The luckless cowhand yelled and clutched at a shattered arm. He almost fell from his saddle as his mount plunged against the haul of reins, and as shock took over he was flung to the packed earth of the yard. He rolled and squirmed, swearing all the while, his face running with sweat.

McLowry clattered down the porch steps and raked his smoking revolver over the remaining three. He had been forced to cross the divide and was ready now to do battle to the bitter end.

"Anybody else wants to buy cards, do it now," he snarled from peeled back lips. "Otherwise, gather your pard up and get the hell out of here. You, Calkin," he spat with brimming venom, "I'd admire to see you make one more bad move so I can drill you square."

Suddenly the whole balance of authority had tilted the other way.

None of Calkin's companions was willing to share the fate of the man on the ground. Calkin himself looked as though he might make one final try to assert the power of the Collins empire. His eyes had taken on a yellowish glow and his fingers itched to do something positive about this upstart who had drifted on to the Anvil Mesa country. He locked gazes with McLowry for the space of ten seconds, read what his fate would be if he pushed his luck too far. He shuddered involuntarily.

"Get Gus on to his horse," he snapped at the others.

McLowry stood back while the wounded cowhand was bundled on to his saddle and the pot-bellied rider led the way out under the hanging Anvil sign. The others went after him, the wounded one continuing to swear and groan. Deke Calkin swung his horse about and made a chopping motion with his right hand. He directed the gesture at Clem Sanderson.

"You're done, Clem . . . done!"

Sanderson unleashed a rifle shot that sent slivers dancing from the gate-post and caused Calkin's horse to break into a mad gallop. Soon the four Spilt C men were pounding along the avenue of cottonwoods, heading for the open range.

McLowry followed their shadows through the interlacing leaves and branches, and when he could no longer see them he canted his head until he was sure they had reached the river and intended going on. Faint curses drifted back to him, angry remonstrations. When he finally replaced the spent shell in his gun and turned to Clem Sanderson and the white-faced Jenny who was framed in the doorway of the house there was a glint of amusement in his eyes.

Sanderson was laughing now, gustily, heartily, losing his breath and then going into another guffaw. He finished up wiping his eyes with a kerchief. McLowry grinned at him, clucked his tongue.

"Last gent I saw hee-hawing like a mule nearly tricked himself into a stroke."

"Hell, I don't care, boy," the rancher panted. "It would be well worth it. See how that damn Deke tucked his tail down? See that Gus Harper trying to keep his busted arm in one piece? Why, even Emmet couldn't have done better." He turned to Jenny. "Say, honey, what did you think of the show? Did you ever see the likes of it?"

The stricken look on the girl's face had a sobering effect on McLowry. She appeared more worried than ever, and there was something akin to accusation in the stare she bent on him. He mounted the porch steps, stood before her.

"You didn't really go along with my play. Jenny, did you?"

"Oh, Frank, I'm not saying they didn't deserve it. I'm not saying you aren't brave. But — but Emmet was brave like that. So were the other men who worked for us. But a bullet in the dark can kill a brave man as easily as a coward. So we haven't really won anything."

McLowry bit his underlip. She had something there, of course. "Maybe you're right," he conceded. "But I figure they'll think twice before riding this way again."

"Don't be too sure of that. I know Deke Calkin, and he simply won't stand for being humiliated. I wouldn't be surprised if he pretended to leave, and then circled back. He might lie up somewhere close until he sees his chance."

"You're right," McLowry agreed. "Very well then, I'll go have a look-see."

He swung away to the corral, not heeding Clem Sanderson's call to hold on, that of course Calkin would keep going until he had reported to his boss. He saddled quickly and loped across the yard, galloping through the gateway and angling out for the cottonwoods. He slowed on reaching the avenue and took it carefully until he reached the river. Hoofprints showed where the Split C riders had forded. He crossed the White and rode cautiously until he gained the open country. Yonder were three riders, streaking into the northwest, the fourth man lagging behind, crouched over his pommel.

McLowry hauled in and wondered what kind of a hurricane he had brought on himself. There would be repercussions, of course. From now on Deke Calkin would be gunning for him, and the man he had wounded would be on his trail as soon as he was fit again. But Calkin had needled him the way he had spoken of Emmet, and the sooner the whole business was out in the open the sooner he might get a chance to even the score for his brother.

Eventually the Split C men receded into the distance and then vanished altogether. McLowry forced himself to relax, to let the tingle die out of his nerves. He was fashioning a cigarette, one leg hooked around his saddle-horn, when he heard hoofbeats pounding up in his rear. It turned out to be Jenny Sanderson on a spirited pony. Her face was flushed and her eyes retained that glint of apprehension as she reined in beside him.

"You should have stayed with your dad."

"Dad can look after himself. Have they really gone?"

"They've lit out anyhow, but maybe just for the time being."

"You expect them to come back when they lick their wounds?"

"I reckon so," he answered with a little shrug.

"They'll come when it's dark," she predicted worriedly. "Possibly tonight. Or Marve might not wait until then: he might send a bigger bunch of his men. He might even come himself."

"That would suit me just fine," McLowry responded with wicked relish.

"Then — then you intend to stay at the ranch until morning?"

He had not really decided on this,

but the note of hope in the girl's voice pleased him, and he nodded.

"I'll have to hear what your dad says first."

"He'll agree, of course. He'll be glad to have you, Frank."

They rode back to the ranch buildings together and Clem Sanderson watched them without commenting as they crossed the yard and went on to the corral. McLowry was thoughtful as he stripped his own horse and the pony. He was so preoccupied that he jerked when the girl laughed softly.

"What's so funny?"

"Nothing. It's such a change having a man do that for me."

"Take care of your pony?" A smile broke through. "It's a pleasure, I'm sure, Miss Sanderson, he said with mock formality."

They rounded the end of the house together, and it was plain that Clem Sanderson had been waiting impatiently. Still, he refrained from firing questions until McLowry had sunk down on the bench beside him. Then, tentatively: "I figured you were heading out?"

"Say the word." McLowry squinted against a blade of sunlight slanting through a gap in the overhang. "I can drift any time you like."

The older man heaved a sigh. "It wouldn't be fair to keep you, Frank. It's different for me and Jenny. Split C knows where we are and that we aim to stay. They wouldn't dare stoop to — to anything really mean."

"Who are you trying to fool, Clem?" McLowry queried with a wry grin. "You're not fooling me, for a start."

"So what do you want to do?"

"I'd like to hang around for a while if you've no objections. Maybe until you're well enough to straddle a horse again."

"There's no guarantee when that'll be."

"I haven't had anything guaranteed to me in my whole life. Look, I'll put my cards on the table, Clem. You need men to work your cattle.

Without enough help it's only a matter of time before you go under, even if Marve Collins never bothers you again. You need a crew, mister, a tough crew that'll stick, no matter what."

"Easier said than done," the other snorted. "Where do I get a crew?"

"It might be managed. But for the time being I need a base, so staying here will benefit you. The sheriff has placed Broken Horn out of bounds to me. Anvil Mesa's smack dab in the centre of everything, and that's where I need to be. So what do you say?"

"Hell, Frank, there's nothing I'd like better than to have you working for me. I'm not broke, by any means. I've made money here, but I'd sacrifice it all if I could make Anvil a brand to be reckoned with again. But you must think of the danger, boy."

"I've thought plenty about it, Clem."

"And you're not scared?"

"Well, the way I see it . . . " McLowry explained with a grin " . . . If Jenny can face up to whatever Collins is liable to throw at this place, then I guess I can, too."

Even this was not enough to satisfy Clem Sanderson. "I'm not so sure that Jenny would be sold on the idea of you working for us, Frank. Even though she might say different. You see, she never really got over Emmet. Your brother was a grand fella to have around, and I believe he and Jenny would have finished up getting married and taking over the ranch eventually. Apart from all that, his killing lies on my conscience like lead. If he'd quit when the rest of the crew quit, your brother would be alive right now."

McLowry averted his gaze from the pain in the man's eyes. He said gruffly: "That sort of thinking gets a man nowhere, Clem. Emmet did what he wanted to do. Nobody forced him. He had obligations here, and if he'd turned his back on you and Jenny when you needed him most he wouldn't have been much of a man."

"Well, by hell, Emmet McLowry was all man, mister!"

"He'd be pleased to hear you say that," McLowry said quietly. He placed his hand on the rancher's shoulder. "So where do I fit in? Do you let me pitch my tent on your ranch or do I move on out to the brush?"

"All depends on Jenny now, Frank. Go inside, and — "

"I'm right here, Dad," the girl said from the doorway. "If Frank is really determined to fight Split C I don't intend to stop him. Frank, you're welcome to Anvil for as long as you wish to stay."

At which Clem Sanderson chuckled and stuck out a big hand. "All right, *hombre*, shake. You've got yourself a deal."

5

ONE of the first tasks McLowry set himself was the renovation of the bunkhouse. Disuse and neglect were fast leaving their marks on everything. He cleared out the mice that had taken up quarters and killed a rattlesnake which disputed his intrusion in no uncertain manner. This was the initial step — providing a berth to sleep in. It gave him a certain insulation and independence that he considered necessary. Sanderson had invited him to make his home in a spare room of the main building, but he refused on the grounds that the bunkhouse must be made habitable if they were to hire a crew.

There was paint in the store-house, green and red, and he used it liberally when the dust and the unwanted denizens had been shifted and the bunks straightened and patched to his satisfaction.

This took a couple of days, and during that time the Anvil ranch had no visitors. Their fears of another call from Deke Calkin or Marve Collins himself failed to materialize. When the bunkhouse was finished McLowry brought Jenny on a tour of inspection, and the girl's warm appreciation of his efforts was ample reward.

He addressed himself to the main building next, armed with hammer, saw and nails, and afterwards with tar and paint. The barn followed, and the outhouses, then the corral fencing. Shaky posts were rooted and made firm and new ones planted. By the end of his first week in the ranch it looked an entirely different place.

As well as all this, McLowry made excursions with Jenny to see to the cattle grazing out on the range. Here, also, were all the tell-tale signs of neglect. Some of the stock had wandered far from home graze, and while they did what they could, the task of caring for a herd of this size — quite apart from keeping it under observation — was virtually impossible. As things stood, everything was being left to chance. Should a band of rustlers decide to make a steal there was very little that could be done about it. In the evenings after supper, McLowry usually rolled into his bunk, totally exhausted, and slept until dawn.

Clem Sanderson was loud in his praise of the work the new man was putting in. He insisted on Jenny and McLowry supporting him between them while he tried to coax life back into his legs. McLowry's zeal seemed to have inspired the rancher, opened a new prospect that he viewed with hope and enthusiasm.

"We'll make her boom, Frank," he crowed. "You and me and Jenny. You can have a job here for life if you want it and can get a new crew."

"Hold your horses, old-timer," McLowry cautioned. "Who said I'd be staying for keeps? What happens if I take itchy feet and decide to drift?"

Sanderson tried to hide his disappointment, but then he challenged; "But I figured you wanted to find out who killed Emmet. Have you changed your mind?"

"Of course I haven't. And maybe I know already who put Emmet out of the way. From what you tell me, Emmet was a thorn in Marve Collins' side. So it just had to be Collins himself or one of his hardcases."

"So what do you intend to do about it? You're only one man, remember, and that crowd could pick you off from ambush any time they like."

"I need a while longer to figure it out," McLowry told him. "I want to be able to jump when I have to. In the meantime, though, I'll do what I can to make a go of this place."

"It's all I can ask," the rancher said philosophically. "But I just hope I'm not helping you to dig your grave, Frank." He brightened, forced a grin.

"At least we know where we stand. Now, you mentioned trying to round up some cowhands . . . Any ideas?"

"One or two maybe. What are the chances of getting men in Broken Horn?"

"It might be the best place to start looking. The town gets its share of drifters. Some of them might jump at the chance of a job."

"Loafers don't interest me much," McLowry said musingly. "I'd like men we can depend on, men who won't run at the sound of a gunshot. What happened to most of your old hands?"

"Scattered, I'd say. Anyhow I don't think they'd come back to stand up to Split C. They had enough of that. In fact, a couple of my hands got berths with Collins, cuss them."

McLowry made a decision. "All right then. I'll ride into Broken Horn and have a look around."

"But you said the sheriff read the riot act to you."

"Sure, he did. But I don't recall

breaking any laws when I was there. Anyhow, I'll have to risk visiting town some time, so it might as well be now."

* * *

He set off in the early afternoon of that day, riding his black horse and armed with his Colt, Winchester and an ample supply of shells. Jenny had appeared worried about his plan and protested to her father, and when Clem Sanderson just shrugged and smiled, the girl hurried outside to call on McLowry as he rode out of the yard.

"Frank, are you sure you know what you're doing? Don't forget what already happened to two of our men as well as Emmet being killed."

"I'm not forgetting anything, ma'am," he assured her gravely. "And don't you worry your pretty head. Look after your dad and try to keep him from doing anything rash if Split C pays a visit."

He took her outstretched fingers and

squeezed them before going on through the gateway. He glanced back once to see her standing there. She raised her hand and he acknowledged the salute. A vision of her stayed with him, clear and sharply etched, until he crossed the river and struck out over the grass.

Now he tried to clear his mind so that he would be on the alert for any sign of danger. During the past week he had been plagued with the notion that curious eyes were watching everything that went on at Anvil. He had never seen anything to justify his anxiety, and he had refrained from mentioning his hunch to Sanderson or his daughter. But years of experience had honed his senses and instincts to a fine edge that could usually be relied on.

He had travelled about three miles from Anvil headquarters when he spotted a horseman far out on his left, and in a short time it became obvious that the rider was keeping him under surveillance. The annoying part of it was that the horseman made no effort to disguise what he was doing. They rode along, almost on a parallel, the stranger slouched slackly in his saddle, apparently casual and uncaring. He stopped once and McLowry guessed he was watering his horse. McLowry took the opportunity to quicken the pace of the black. The other rider was soon on the move again, making haste now to recover his position on McLowry's flank.

Initially, McLowry was inclined to shrug off the manoeuvre, seeing it as a far from subtle attempt to rattle his nerves. But as another couple of miles went by with the unknown rider maintaining his position, he felt a surge of slow anger pulsing into his bloodstream.

It looked as if Split C meant to make it clear that his every movement was being watched and noted, that no matter what he did, Marve Collins could keep track of him. McLowry saw it as a gesture of defiance and warning. They were telling him that he might have safe passage if he pulled out of the country at once, but if he insisted in poking his nose in where it wasn't wanted then he must accept the consequences.

Anvil Mesa was a long way behind him now, and the wilderness of rocks that he would have to negotiate loomed up ahead, stark and forbidding. If the rider out there intended to intercept him he would have to make his play shortly.

No sooner had the thought crossed his mind than a rifle cracked viciously and a heavy bullet whined away in front of him, startling the black so that he had to drag hard on the reins. He was on the ground when the second shot came, and he swung about to get a glimpse of the marksman. It was as if the land had swallowed him and those shots had been the outcome of a heated imagination.

But it was plain to see what had happened: the horseman had bided his time until he reached an area where the earth billowed and ran into numerous folds and hollows. McLowry sank down in the long grass, his own rifle snugged in at his shoulder. He batted his hat up a little to give him a wider field of vision. There was nothing to be seen, however.

Ten minutes dragged by. A sharp breeze rippled through the grass and sage. A tangy scent came to his nostrils. A clump of gnarled cedars on his left looked inviting to McLowry, and he wondered what would happen if he ventured into the open and made a quick run for it. The black had trotted off a distance behind him and was whickering nervously, as though wishing to tell him something.

A sudden, low drumming of hoofbeats travelled over the billows to his ears and he rose to his knees in order to get a better look. The marksman, whoever he was, had broken out of his covert. He triggered a single shot before going into flight.

McLowry sent an answering shot

through the waving grass, then lunged upright and hurried to his horse. In the saddle, he angled across the face of a steep cliff and came out on a pitching slope that gave him a brief view of the ambusher. He was galloping along a narrow track that described a sinuous course among the sandstone walls and, even as McLowry paused to stare, he vanished once more.

McLowry's mouth puckered in a tight grin. He wiped his brow and considered the lay of the land. The rifleman would know every nook and cranny, while he knew practically nothing about the geography of the country. A hawk hovered in the heavens above him, dropped a distance and switched direction, then wheeled on over a craggy rim. The land was silent, the heat oppressive. A cloud of flies found him and he batted them off.

Why had the rifleman behaved in that manner, he wondered. Why had he shown himself — flaunted himself would describe it better — then sent off those few shots before doing his disappearing trick? There was no apparent logic in the manoeuvre, unless . . .

That was when another idea suggested itself. McLowry had a quick vision of a fisherman with his baited line trailing the water; was that what the ambusher had been doing — playing his bait in such a way that he would lure Emmet McLowry's brother into this rock fastness?

"Well, there's nothing much to be gained by going after him," he mused, fingering out his tobacco sack. "The gent just made his play and then went shy on me."

He considered the possibility of other Split C men lurking in the vicinity — granting that the bushwhacker rode under Marve Collins' brand. At this very minute there could be a dozen eyes watching him, rifles and six-guns could be trained on him, waiting for the right moment to cut him down. Wounding Gus Harper would make them all the more eager to nail him.

He cuffed his brow again, swallowed thickly. He flung the cigarette makings from him. He was getting jittery, ready to jump at his own shadow. And maybe that was what the man who had been tracking him hoped to accomplish.

At length he decided to retrace his way along the base of the cliff until he hit the trail that would lead him to Broken Horn. When he reached the stage road that linked Broken Horn with Gopher Flats he turned into the east, relaxing a little. Still, as he drew closer to the town he was aware of a new tension building in him.

Broken Horn was bustling with life, and people looked as if they were too busy with their own affairs to bother with the cowhand riding down the main street on his black horse. As he cut out for the direction of the livery, McLowry kept scanning the boardwalks for Sheriff Dan Bennet or his deputy, but he saw no sign of them.

The hostler recognized him as the stranger Dan Bennet had seen fit to escort out of town, and his worried frown soon turned into an amused smile. "Something told me you were the kind of bird that wouldn't scare easy," he observed. "How are you, mister?"

"Can't complain, I guess," McLowry responded cheerfully. "Don't mind if I leave my nag here?"

"Help yourself. But I'd better warn you about the sheriff — "

"You don't have to," McLowry interjected. "Sure, he threw me out, and he might get around to making a habit of it. But if I'd come in wearing a Split C brand, things might have been different, huh?"

"Say, you're catching on pretty fast," the other chuckled.

"I'm catching on." McLowry began stripping Blackie and the hostler fell silent. He picked up a hay-fork and began spreading straw around. He was plainly tickled by the big man's nerve.

112

Or maybe he thought that McLowry didn't have enough sense to know what was good for him. McLowry decided to push his luck a little. "I hear Marve Collins has this country just about wrapped up. Doesn't that kind of power worry you none?"

He was subjected to a hard look while the hostler leaned on the handle of his fork and scratched his scrawny neck. He spat deliberately, rubbed his nose. "Why should it bother me?" he countered. "I mind my own business and let other folks mind theirs."

McLowry allowed a wintry smile to lighten his eyes. "You figure you're a pretty smart old coot, don't you?"

"Never said I was smart."

"Careful?"

"Want me to give your nag a rub down and grain him?"

McLowry made an elaborate display of resigning himself to defeat. Then he mustered another smile. "Thanks, pard. Do that. I hope you don't take offence at anything I said."

"No sir, mister. Got me a hide that'd turn this here fork."

McLowry went back to the street and lingered at a corner where he could view the traffic eddying to and fro. Broken Horn was a thriving cow town, without doubt, and there were bound to be men around who would welcome the chance of a job with a steady wage. He hadn't quite made up his mind what he would do if he happened to run into Dan Bennet or his deputy, Jed Deakin.

He pushed through the ornate swing-doors of a saloon that was doing quite a trade and reflected over a cool beer. It was too early in the day for the card-sharps to be in evidence, but the clicking and clacking of billiard balls attracted him to a table in one end of the room, and he took his beer across to watch. Two cowhands were sending the balls around the table with no regard for rules or restrictions, and the performance brought a faint smile to his mouth.

The waddies soon tired, and the blond youngster who had been standing beside McLowry, and who had noticed his unspoken wry amusement, begged his pardon.

"You look like a gent who could use a cue the way it ought to be used, sir."

"Well, that just proves you should never go by looks," McLowry grinned. "I haven't played in a mighty long time."

"Now ain't that the oldest excuse in the world! Let's bang 'em around if it's nothing else."

"Suits me," McLowry said with a shrug.

The outcome was that he spent a pleasant half-hour on the table. The youngster was quite adept and offered worthy challenge to McLowry's unconscious — but nevertheless somewhat smug — air of authority. Their adherence to the rules of the game and their evident skill soon drew attention. This, in turn, had the effect of triggering a little adrenalin into McLowry's bloodstream. He beat the blond by a few points, and when the cues were racked, the youngster laughed and shook his hand with mock solemnity.

"A pleasure playing with you, suh. But don't you think that old table ain't good for much else but sleeping on?"

"It must be the oldest there is around," McLowry drawled. "But you sure ain't the oldest piece of furniture around, mister."

"Name's Eagen," the other offered. "Marty's the front part of the handle. Late of points south." His voice dropped and his blue eyes twinkled. "Pretty far south, at that. Say, would you let me buy you a drink?"

"If you let me buy you a chaser. And my handle's Frank McLowry."

"My rule is loser pays, Frank. But I'm willing to bend it a mite on this occasion."

Over at the counter, McLowry called for beer and Marty Eagen asked for the same. "Ain't being stingy," the youngster explained. "Just don't cotton much to the red-eyed stuff."

They chatted in generalities that presently began to take on a more personal quality. Eagen had been 'down south for a spell. Way down south,' which McLowry deduced as embracing that part of the world on the other side of the Rio Grande. He had remained there until the indiscretion responsible for him making the trip had dimmed in certain memories.

"Figure to hunt me up a job in these parts," he added. "Was talking to a big fella earlier. Worked for Split C, he said. Told me I'd find a berth at the Collins outfit out on White River. Know where it is?"

McLowry frowned and sloshed the beer dregs around in the bottom of his glass. "Got a rough idea," he said shortly.

"Beg pardon, suh, but do you know something about that outfit I maybe ought to hear about?"

"No, don't get me wrong . . . I'm not saying the Collins spread wouldn't fill the bill for you. But I could make you an offer myself if you're interested."

"Hey, what about that now! Say, you don't strike me like a rancher. Begging your pardon, Frank, if I've tramped on a corn."

"No, it's all right. I'm not a rancher, as it happens. Look . . . have you got the time to listen to what I'm up to? If you don't like the idea, all you have to do is say so."

"Hell, I've all the time in the world, Frank." The blond youngster grinned ingenuously. "Go ahead and shoot. But what say we take the weight off'n our legs while we palaver? You stake your claim to yon table and I'll get us another beer."

And that was how Frank McLowry signed up his first recruit for Clem Sanderson's Anvil brand. McLowry made no attempt to paint over the cracks or offer golden rewards. He explained the situation exactly as it was, and when he had finished Marty Eagen flashed his white teeth in appreciation.

"Darn it, that sounds like real fun. So instead of going to work for this Split C spread, I might end up fighting them."

"I'd better warn you that it won't be much of a joke if Collins gets rough," McLowry warned. "I hear he can be real mean when he feels like it."

"Collins doesn't scare me, Frank. Say, I can't wait to clap my eyes on this Miss Jenny you talk about. I'd sure like to — " He broke off at the change in McLowry's expression, then chuckled and leaned over to slap the big man's shoulder. "Don't worry none, pard. When I come on a place that's got claim markers I keep my hands off."

"You're just plain loco," McLowry retorted, trying to shield his confusion.

"That's me with bells on, Frank. But being plain loco's what makes life so hell-awful interesting, I reckon. And this Sanderson gentleman must figure you for quite a *hombre* when he trusts you like this."

"Not so you'd notice. Now quit trying to make me blush. I haven't blushed since I saw that lady kick her heels up at the playhouse in Dodge. I was just fourteen or so, and I've never been able to look a woman straight in the face since."

McLowry was pleased with his acquisition. And the fact that he had plucked Marty Eagen from the open arms of Split C added something special to the deal. He left the youngster — Eagen was just about eighteen or nineteen — with the understanding that he would pick him up at the livery stable in the morning.

He visited the other saloons, drinking sparingly, not drinking at all where thumbing his nose at etiquette would not be noticed. He mingled with the customers, his continued aim the signing up of likely riders. He ventured a question to a bartender in the Sage Saloon who, in turn, pointed out a disconsolate-looking individual at the end of the bar.

"Never been in here before. Just been cleaned out at poker. Did you say you're signing for the Anvil outfit? Then you must know Clem Sanderson that owns — "

"I know him," McLowry interrupted with a faint smile. "Thanks for the help."

He moved along the counter so that he might have an opportunity to appraise the dismal cowhand. He noticed that he was short and tubby, and that he actually did appear to be on the point of despair as he gazed broodingly into his empty glass.

McLowry circled him and came in at his side. "Sorry if I pushed," he apologised.

He was subjected to a jaundiced scrutiny, but the belligerence on the round face soon melted before McLowry's guileless smile.

"Forget it, mister. I might as well get used to being pushed around. Tramped on, too, maybe. They say the local law just loves vagrants."

"Vagrant?" McLowry echoed with affected amazement. "I took you for a cowpoke straight off. Vagrant by preference or circumstance?"

"Huh?" The tubby man glared suspiciously before the gist of the remark registered. "Oh, I was a cowpoke right enough," he confided. "But right now I'm no higher than a gopher's fetlock. Just got rid of the finest little roan in Carver County. All on account of three lousy kings! Three kings and a pair of tens. Can you beat it, mister?"

"Sounds like a nice hand to me. The other gent hold aces?"

"It wasn't my hand, it was Keating's. I figured that bird for a sharp soon as he showed up. Should have packed when he sat down."

"Too bad," McLowry commiserated. "So Keating won your wad? Reckon that means you're broke?"

"Way, way down broke, Jack. But I ain't crying on account of losing my money. It's that damn Keating that sticks in my craw. I reckon I might hunt him up and — "

"He's bound to blow your head off," McLowry observed with a straight face. "Look, forget about Keating for a minute. Do you need a job?"

"A job? You mean work, don't you? And just when I figured to go on a spree . . . Say, you're not planning on robbing a bank or something like that, Jack? I draw the line at robbing banks."

"I'm talking about singing beeves to sleep at night," McLowry told him. "And my name isn't Jack: it's Frank McLowry."

"Shucks, mister, I'm powerful sorry. You look like a Jack I used to know. But when I drink too much everybody looks like Jack, and I — think I'm kind of — drunk right now. Don't go away! You mentioned a job? A riding job? I hear a man can be hung or shot dead for just riding a horse with the wrong brand on it."

"Riding under *this* brand might get you shot, fella," McLowry warned him. "But if you're in town at dawn, and cold sober, I'll talk to you and sign you on. If you want to join the outfit that *does* the shooting, hunt up Marve Collins' Split C outfit."

"Say, a man told me that was Keating's outfit! Work with a cardsharp like Keating? Not on your life, mister."

"I'm collecting a gent at the livery in the morning," McLowry said. "Be there if you want a job at Anvil Mesa ranch. I'll stake you to a bronc, deductible from your pay."

The tubby man's name was Dobe Jenkins. He wanted to hear more, but McLowry had other things to do, and he soon left the saloon. He was well pleased with himself at this juncture. Of course, there was the risk of Eagen and Jenkins changing their minds about working for Clem Sanderson, especially when they had time to think about the possible hazards. But it was a risk he had to take.

He finished the day off by hiring a cowhand who had recently quit Split C after a row with Collins' foreman, Brin Eckols. This rider was about thirty, and he struck McLowry favourably. His name was Nate Bream, and he claimed that all he wanted was a chance to hit back at Collins' outfit.

"They're a pack of coyotes," he said vehemently. "I been there six months and I know how they work. They scared blazes out of a homesteader that had a woman and three kids."

"What was your fight with Eckols over?" McLowry queried.

"A girl I met in Gopher Flats. Brin was jealous, bragged about how he knew Maggie. He knew her just too damn well to be telling the truth. I pasted him and got a beefing from the boss. Then I quit."

"I guess you know what Collins thinks of Anvil?"

"Sure, I do. He's had his eye on that place for a long time. He was after the Sanderson girl, too, so they tell me. But he couldn't get her. Now he's just about ruined old Clem. But that doesn't scare me none at all, McLowry. All I want is to get a crack at them."

"You'd have to hold your temper, do what you're told. And even then you might get yourself killed."

"So what? I bet I'll do some killing myself if I have to."

McLowry was not entirely happy about taking on Nate Bream. It might give Split C additional reason for harrying Clem Sanderson. But then, he reflected wryly, it wasn't a cosy party he was planning: it was the reorganisation of a cattle outfit. And that would mean having men on the payroll who would stand up to whatever Marve Collins threw at them.

It was approaching dusk when he

wended his way towards the hotel. He was passing the darkened doorway of a store when someone hailed him.

"Hey, you there, McLowry . . . " Sheriff Dan Bennet.

6

TENSION gripped McLowry, and for a brief moment he wondered if the sheriff had been following him around and knew what he was up to. Bennet's features were warped in a bleak smile that was in no wise encouraging.

"Hello, Sheriff. Guess you're surprised to find me in town?"

"Not so you'd notice," Bennet replied with a trace of smugness in his tone. "As a matter of fact Jed Deakin's been keeping an eye on you since you arrived."

McLowry's brows arched quizzically. "That says I must be an interesting specimen, I guess."

"Interesting enough. And the fact that you appear to have lost your memory makes me hanker to take a closer look at you. Let's stroll along here," he added abruptly and started walking.

If he expected the tall man to comply immediately he was disappointed. McLowry hesitated, bristling, but then he shrugged and fell into step with the star-packer. Bennet said nothing more until they had worked over a fairly wide intersection that had mounds of crusted dust piled up where wheel marks angled one way or another into three converging streets. When they reached the opposite boardwalk the sheriff halted and pushed his hat up from his forehead.

"I don't think folks around here would call me a hard man, mister," was his puzzling preamble. "But let's be straightforward about the whole matter. You came here to make good for your brother's death — Please don't interrupt! I reckon you've got a good reason to carry a chip on your shoulder. But hunting killers and such is a job for the law. You understand that, I guess?"

"Perfectly," McLowry said curtly with a dip of the head. "But you didn't catch Emmet's killer, Sheriff."

"Now take it easy, bub, take it easy!"

It occurred to McLowry that Dan Bennet had set out to placate him, but that his reaction had caused the lawman to believe he was wasting his time. He waited patiently while Bennet continued.

"Now, I told you to leave this town for your own good. I thought you might have enough sense to see that I meant what I said. But what do we find you doing?" He paused to allow the enormity of the situation to register fully. "You damn well start a recruiting campaign for Clem Sanderson's Anvil outfit. Now where's the sense in trying to give Sanderson a false sense of security? Sanderson knows he's up against a brick wall, and you're a bigger fool than he is if you can't see that for yourself. Why hire workers for a spread that's going to fall anyhow?"

McLowry choked back a sharp retort and studied the man in the gathering shadows. "Why are you so interested in Anvil at all, Sheriff?" he queried. "Is it on account of my brother getting killed while working for Sanderson? Is it because two Anvil men were bushwhacked by gutless cowards and the rest decided to quit before they got the same medicine?"

"Now you hold it right there, damn you," Dan Bennet growled. "Just who in blazes do you think you are?"

"Right now I'm just a gent called Frank McLowry," was the terse response. "I had a brother who got himself killed by those same cowards, and I'm going to find out who the rats are. I reckon that should do for the time being."

Bennet pulled a hard breath through his teeth. His dark eyes glittered like fireflies. He stabbed a blunt finger for emphasis. "You'd better get something through your head, sonny. You're sitting on a keg of dynamite. It could blow you to kingdom-come at any minute. I don't want another killing on my hands."

"And I'd say you're not overly anxious to tramp on Marve Collins' toes either."

He was prepared for anything but the sheriff striking him. The openhanded cuff took him on the jaw and sent his head rocking back on his shoulders. McLowry straightened, his own eyes fiery, his mouth a fine, tight line. He breathed shallowly, fighting to control the fury that swirled through him.

"Don't ever do that again, mister," he hissed. "Sheriff or not, I'll beat your skull into pulp."

"Why you — "

"I'm telling you, you bag of wind," McLowry insisted. "I don't take kindly to being slapped down. I've seen men killed for less."

The lawman took a step towards him, froze. The shadows were deepening. Something in the way the tall man stood, in the way he hunched his shoulders slightly, in the paleness of

132

his face in the gloom, convinced Dan Bennet that he, rather than McLowry, would be lighting a dynamite fuse if he attempted to bully Emmet's brother.

"I should run you in right now," he blustered.

"You could try it, mister. But I mightn't take kindly to that sort of treatment either."

Just then a figure shifted through the darkness, having detached itself from a doorway on the corner. McLowry soon recognized the lanky, stoop-shouldered man. Dan Bennet wheeled to peer at the newcomer.

"That you, Jed?" His tone trembled with relief.

"It's me, Dan. What's the bother? Say . . . is that our friend again?"

"It's him all right," the lawman spat. "Getting uppity. I'm trying to make up my mind what I ought to do with him — for the good of his own health."

"Well, you told him to stay out of your bailiwick, didn't you? And here he is, large as life, and stirring up heaven knows what. Couldn't you rate that as contempt, maybe?"

"Maybe," Bennet agreed thinly. "But I don't think I'll bother. I've a strong hunch that Mr McLowry here is pretty busy at the minute digging a deep hole for himself."

"It'll be a real big one," McLowry scowled. "Big enough to hold any sidewinder who figures he's smart enough to nail me from behind."

His remark served to stretch the tension between them. The very air seemed to throb with the potential for menace. The lawmen exchanged secret glances, and McLowry noted that this end of the town was deserted. In spite of his spindly frame, Jed Deakin might manage to give a fair account of himself in a set-to. As for Dan Bennet himself, he had been brought up in the belief and conviction that he must fight tooth and nail for whatever he hoped to achieve. He was tough and strong, and he was capable of giving a man a bad mauling.

Jed Deakin appeared to read the thoughts flitting through McLowry's mind and to have decided to keep up the pressure.

"We could make him want to leave town, Dan," he suggested with a downward twist to his mouth. "What about it?"

"That's an idea, Jed," Bennet murmured. "A real good idea."

"An idea that could get you into a heap of trouble," McLowry told them. He left a space between them, spread his elbows in the manner of an eagle spreading its wings preparatory to flight or attack. "But if you really want it that way, let's give it a whirl."

Jed Deakin's wolfish grin vanished and he gave his hat brim a tug down on his forehead. He glanced along the street, a furtive animal of prey now rather than a peace officer. Piano music drifted faintly from a saloon far down the avenue. They heard someone laugh. A dog barked resentfully at the rising moon. The three men were insulated in a tension that had grown to the pitch where something just had to give.

McLowry was leaning forward, balanced on the balls of his feet, trying to watch both men at the same time.

Jed Deakin said urgently to Dan Bennet: "Are you ready?"

And that was the moment when the tension broke and the wind ran out of the sheriff in a ragged sigh. He might have been giving a belated expression to some pain that plagued him.

"Hold it," he cried hoarsely. "Are you crazy, Jed? What do you figure this is?"

"But if you don — "

"Shut up," the sheriff admonished sharply. He sounded disgusted with the whole business. He cleared his throat loudly and spat. A shiver appeared to run over him, freeing him from something he would have regretted. He said to McLowry: "You'd better watch your step. I'm not fooling now. I mean it, friend."

"Sure . . . "

McLowry backed on off, watching the deputy rather than his boss. He left the planking and backed on through the road dust. It seemed a long time before the darkness swallowed the two men standing yonder. He turned abruptly and began walking swiftly. He heard their voices behind him, hoarse, argumentative. He kept walking. Someone stepped out of an alley and he drove for his gun. The man rocked up on his heels, started to lift his arms. He laughed shakily as McLowry shoved the revolver away, cursing, cold sweat rolling down his brow. He broke into a run before the man had a chance to see him clearly and perhaps remember him later.

He found the hotel and booked a room. He was surprised to discover how hungry he was and he ate his supper with relish. He bought a handful of cigars at the counter and went back into the street. He fired one of the tobacco sticks and angled over the road. He skirted the railroad station and the stockyards, seeing the pens heaving with cattle and the shadowy forms of a couple of guards. The burning tips of cigarettes marked their positions clearly. Next, he made his way to the far end of town, left the outskirts, and hauled up when he noticed a pale glow in the window of Pedro Juarez's shack.

He knocked on the door and was greeted by a cautious Juarez. "*Quien es?*"

"Frank McLowry, Pedro. Could I speak with you?"

"It is getting late, señor — "

McLowry gnashed his teeth. Was the Mexican's backbone beginning to wilt as well?

"Too late to speak with an *amigo*?"

He heard a sigh, a chain being unhooked. The door opened. A dimly burning lantern hung from the ceiling. The small stove glowed. There was a smell of chicory, garlic. McLowry stared at a youthful Mexican on a stool by the stove.

"Come in, Señor McLowry."

The Mexican rose silently. He was fine-featured, sloe-eyed, with a mop of black hair that was all curls, tight-rolled, and which bobbed when he moved.

"This is Esteban, señor. My nephew who is visiting me. Esteban, meet Señor McLowry."

"I am honoured, señor," Esteban murmured in good English. He bowed his head slightly. McLowry did likewise and extended his hand.

"There is no need to leave, Esteban," he said. "I am not staying." He tugged off his hat, ignored the chair that Juarez drew out for him. Juarez brought a demi-john into view, lifted a tin cup and poured. He handed the cup to McLowry.

"Tequila, *amigo*. *Bueno*."

McLowry sipped and nodded. "You're right at that, pard." He swallowed the drink, feeling the glow rise out of his stomach and bring heat to his face. Juarez and Esteban watched without speaking.

"I'm working for Clem Sanderson's Anvil ranch, Pedro. Thought I should call and thank you for the lead."

The Mexican remained silent, his features inscrutable.

"I found out, too, why Emmet was killed," McLowry went on. "And I'm sure I know who was behind it."

"You are staying in this country then, *amigo*?" Juarez murmured.

"For a while, yes. Sheriff Bennet hasn't bothered you again?"

"No one bothers me, señor."

"Good. Well, I won't keep you, Pedro. Thanks again for everything. Something bothered me though . . . Why didn't you tell me everything in the first place?"

Juarez shrugged. "It does not do to talk too much. My nephew worked for a homesteader named Alturo. Alturo was driven off his land, so — "

"So Esteban is out of a job?"

Esteban grinned. "I will find another. I used to watch sheep for my father. But I would rather work with cattle."

"Well, what about that now! I could use another rider at Anvil. It's really what brought me to town, to hire a crew. How would you feel about going to work for Clem Sanderson?"

Esteban's face lit up. "You mean it, señor?"

"Sure, I do. Do you know how to get to the ranch?"

"I know where it is."

"Be there tomorrow." McLowry smiled. "Well, what about that now! I reckon I've made a day of it after all."

A tear glistened in Pedro's eyes. "You make me very happy, *amigo*. My brother's boy is a good worker. You will not be disappointed."

"I'm sure I won't. Just one thing, Esteban. You understand the kind of trouble we're liable to get from Split C?"

"My brother's boy is brave," Pedro assured him. "Also, he can use a pistol."

"I hope he won't have to use it.

Well, I'll look forward to seeing you, Esteban. Good night, Pedro."

He went back into the darkness, complimenting himself on having called on Juarez at the right time. He struck a match for one of his cigars, then headed back towards the lights of Broken Horn's main street.

★ ★ ★

A man had stalked Frank McLowry to the Mexican's place and remained hidden in the shadows until he emerged. He gave the tall man time to stalk off, then moved cautiously to the small window and peered through a chink in the curtain. He dropped back when the chain rattled, and he watched Esteban come out. The youth and the old man conversed in low-pitched Spanish for a while. They laughed at some joke and bade each other farewell. The door was closed and Esteban went to the rear of the house and broke the hobbles of the horse he had left there.

He was whistling as he mounted lithely and pushed the horse into the gloom and away from the road into Broken Horn. The man in the shadows moved over to the front of the house, paused to look around him. Satisfied that the coast was clear, he rapped on the door with his knuckles.

There was silence for a few moments, then he caught the shuffling of sandalled feet.

"*Quien es?*" The voice was ready, tinged ever so slightly with apprehension.

The stranger growled: "McLowry."

"But I thought you had gone, señor. Have you forgotten something?"

"Sure, Pedro."

The chain clinked; the door opened a fraction, but wide enough for the man to stick his toe into the aperture. He laughed as the Mexican fell back fearfully.

"Señor Calkin . . . But what do you want with me? It is late, and — "

"Shut up," Deke Calkin growled. He threw another probing stare into the shadows behind him; he appeared satisfied. The drumming hooves of Esteban's horse were fast receding into distance.

With a yelp of dismay Pedro dashed to the small bureau against a wall, hauled open a drawer. His fingers were closing on the .44 Remington lodged there when Calkin reached him and clutched his shoulder. He wrenched him away and threw him to the floor.

"Not so fast, greaser." Calkin hefted his own gun menacingly. "Now, talk, and do it hellish quick. What did McLowry want here just then?"

"He — he . . . I do not understand you, señor."

"No? Then maybe this might help." Calkin raked the Mexican's ribs with his boot. Juarez moaned.

"He — will kill — you . . . "

"McLowry? You must be joking, mister. But that shows the way the wind's blowing, doesn't it? You and McLowry are thick, just like I figured. He tells you things and you tell him things. What things, bub?"

"Señor, you are wrong . . . "

"Want to bet on it?" Calkin's strong hand fastened in Juarez's shirt. He hauled the old man to his feet. His breath stank of whisky. His beady eyes gleamed malevolently. "Talk, damn you."

"I — I — He offered Esteban a job, señor. That is all. I swear that is all!"

Calkin frowned, rubbed his chin with the barrel of his revolver. "A job?" He poked the muzzle of the weapon into the old man's midriff. "Well, don't stop when your story's getting interesting, Pop. What sort of job? Where?"

"At Anvil Mesa."

"No fooling?" Calkin chortled. "Well, maybe that figures. McLowry's taking over at the mesa, and he's trying to get a crew together. But we'll fix that coyote's hash, you bet! And anybody else that gets mixed up with him, too."

"You will never get him," Juarez

retorted, stung to angry defiance. "You may have got his brother. But not this one."

"Haw, haw! Ain't that a laugh now? Don't it just beat hell . . . Well, if you want to know, I could have shot him dead when he stepped out there a while back. Only I wanted to hear what he was up to. And what do you know about Emmet McLowry, you filthy beggar?"

"*Nada* . . . "

"*Nada, nada!* You liar. I always figured you for a sneaky spy, Juarez. Now I know. And Marve Collins doesn't care to have gents around that can hurt him. *Sabe?*"

"But I didn't — "

"Don't lie, damn you."

Calkin flung Pedro from him again and the Mexican slammed into the wall and fell. He bent over, moaning, sick and pained. Calkin ran his tongue across his lips, thumbed back the hammer of his Colt. The lamplight glittered on steel as Pedro Juarez lunged

146

up with a cry resembling that of a wounded animal. The knife was leaving his fingers when Calkin triggered. Once, twice, the shots exploded deafeningly. Juarez sagged to his knees, his skinny hands uplifted as if in supplication, then he toppled over in a heap.

Sweat glinted on Deke Calkin's forehead. A thick vein in his temple throbbed. He wiped his brow, swung to the door and drew it open. He peered into the night. It was quiet; nothing stirred. He grinned with his lips peeled back from his teeth, but the lips trembled. A worry was working through his consciousness, trying to reach the surface. He stifled it and ran to where he had left his horse. In the saddle, he hesitated, head raised to catch sound. The only thing he could hear was the wild hammering of his heart. He laughed recklessly and spurred the horse into the moon-dappled shadows.

* * *

The drumming of the shots reached McLowry's ears as he arrived at the outskirts of Broken Horn. He halted, frowning, glancing back in the direction of Pedro's place. Someone emerged from a doorway along the street and followed his stare.

"Sounded like shooting," a fat man with rolled-up sleeves declared.

"Sure did." McLowry made a decision. "Mister, maybe you should fetch the law."

"Think there's trouble?"

"Reckon so."

The man hurried down the road and McLowry swung about and broke into a loose-limbed run. At the same time he picked up the clatter of hoofbeats leaving town and cutting into the north, and he immediately thought of Esteban.

"But it couldn't have been him . . . "

He hauled up at the front of the Juarez house and knew by the way the door hung open that something was badly wrong. Yellow light streamed over the earth in a broad, mottled ribbon, and he fingered out his Colt and called: "You there, Pedro?"

No answer. He approached the door slowly, cautiously. It seemed that Esteban had gone, but where was Juarez?

He eased on into the room, mouthing a curse when he saw old Pedro lying in a pool of blood. He fell to one knee and touched the wrinkled face, the neck. The eyes stared lifelessly. Now he swallowed hard, still thinking about Esteban. Pedro had been shot twice.

He saw the knife then, just inside the talon-twisted fingers, and a scrawl of blood, as though a spider had been crawling through it. He sucked a quick breath when the pieces of the pattern came together. Pedro had lived long enough to leave a clue that might point to his killer.

McLowry brought the lantern from its ceiling hook and held it so that the full glare of the light struck the floor. 'C-a-l', he spelled out. He sat staring at the spidery letters for a while, trying to make sense of them. Then he rose and replaced the lantern on its hook.

"Cal?" he whispered, searching his memory. "Cal who? But maybe that was just part of the name . . . Cal, Cal — I've got it! It just has to be the Split C rider Calkin!"

McLowry breathed slowly through his teeth, remembering the caller out at Anvil Mesa. Yes, killing old Pedro would be right in Calkin's character. Calkin must have seen him calling on Pedro and wondered what was in the wind. He had waited until McLowry and Pedro's nephew had left, then managed to get into the house. Murder! Juarez had tried to protect himself with his knife and had failed.

McLowry heard horses running from the direction of town. It looked as if Sheriff Bennet had lost no time after being alerted. He felt a little anxious now, frightened. Perhaps he should have investigated before summoning the sheriff to the scene. But it was too late to make amends.

Two horses at least thundered up outside and their riders scrambled to the ground. Sheriff Bennet entered, accompanied by someone McLowry had never seen before. The other man was tall, lean, sober-featured. He wore a black hat and frock coat. The mayor, maybe, he hazarded. Someone of importance in Broken Horn for sure.

Dan Bennet threw McLowry a dark look which said that of course it had to be him at the bottom of the wood-pile. He stooped to peer at the dead Mexican, grunted, straightened, and thrust his hat up from his forehead. He said drily to McLowry: "Show me your gun."

"I didn't shoot him."

"Show me your gun."

McLowry handed it over, bristling at the way the lean man was looking down his nose at him. Bennet examined the loads, sniffed the barrel.

"Didn't you have another six-shooter?"

"Just this one." McLowry had difficulty in keeping his temper. He suspected that the sheriff hoped he would do something foolish so that he could make an early arrest. That would probably please the character in the frock coat, whoever he was.

"All right then, friend," the sheriff growled. "Tell me what happened. Juarez is dead and you're right here with him. Can you explain?"

"I was at the edge of town when I heard the shooting," McLowry said tersely. "The man who fetched you can bear me out. It was me who told him to find you." He reached for the lantern once more, and now the stranger spoke for the first time, his voice a sharp, whining rasp. "What are you doing?"

McLowry ignored him. He brought the lantern down and held it close to the floor. "Read what he tried to write," he told Dan Bennet.

The sheriffs jaw dropped in wonder but he stooped over Juarez again.

"Some blood. But what — "

"Now you try," McLowry said to the other man.

The thin, poker-faced individual — whom McLowry was beginning to think could well be the local undertaker — jerked at being forced into active participation. Nevertheless, he moved to a spot where the light threw up the scrawled letters in relief.

"C-o-l or C-a-l," he said. "What do you suppose it indicates, if anything?"

"See if you can figure it out," McLowry urged. "Juarez lived for just long enough to try and give the name of his killer. To me it spells C-a-l, but I'm sure Pedro really meant Calkin."

Bennet's head flashed up, his eyes glittering. "Deke Calkin?"

"The Split C hand," McLowry said. "Who else?"

The sheriff emitted a sharp, derisive laugh. "That's plain ridiculous. Juarez could have meant anything by that, or nothing. A scrawl made by a dying man? It wouldn't stand up anywhere."

153

"Certainly not in a court of law," the frock-coated man said coldly. "By the way, I'm Judge Henry Loftus. I'm in the process of making my circuit."

McLowry's jaw hardened. "It might pay you to stay in these parts for a spell, Judge. This territory sure needs somebody with an open eye and an open mind."

Loftus subjected him to a probing stare that caused McLowry to hope he would never have to face him in a courtroom. "This has always been a rough neck of the woods," the judge observed.

"Do you not agree with what I just said, Judge — about the way the Mexican tried to leave a message?"

"That's where my open mind comes into play, Mr McLowry," was the stiff response.

"I'll hunt up Calkin," Dan Bennet declared. "You keep quiet about this in the meantime, McLowry . . . Now, you'd better get out of here. I know where to find you if I need you."

7

BEFORE he turned in McLowry asked direction to the undertaker's place, and after a good deal of searching he ran the Boothill agent down in a saloon. Oscar Dwire turned out to be pretty drunk, but he was able to grasp what McLowry was driving at and demanded full expense on the spot. He was given half of his fee, the rest to be paid when Frank McLowry was satisfied that Pedro Juarez would get a proper funeral.

Esteban should be notified, of course, as he might want to make his own plans for his uncle's burial, but there was no time to contact him.

McLowry ate a light supper and went straight to his room. The memory of Pedro Juarez lying in a pool of blood plagued him like a fever that was going to be hard to shake off. Nevertheless, as soon as his head hit the pillow he fell into a deep, dreamless sleep and awoke feeling wonderfully refreshed.

He washed and ate breakfast, then made his way through the meagre morning light to the livery. Marty Eagen was squatting against the end of a stall, blowing into a harmonica. The cowhand's face lit up as he scrambled to his feet.

"Well, boss, here I is, fresh and spunky!"

McLowry took Eagen's presence as a good augury. He brought his horse out and saddled up. He was tightening the girth when the tubby Dobe Jenkins appeared, eliciting a crowing noise from Eagen.

"Mr McLowry, are you going to tell me that fat dumpling can actually straddle a bronc?" he queried mischievously.

Jenkins' smile faded before the blond youngster's brashness and he patted his revolver meaningly. "No sass from you, button," he rebuked. "And it'll pay you handsome if you keep that in mind."

McLowry smoothed the situation with a few crisp words, then introduced the men. Eagen was gleeful when he discovered that Jenkins was actually without a horse.

"I guess you know what they say about a gent that'll sell his saddle, Frank. He'll never be worth a damn to nobody."

Eagen's raw humour was fast souring Jenkins, and McLowry saw the makings of a private feud before he even managed to get the men out to Anvil. He would have to tramp on it at once.

"All right, Marty, you've made it plain that you're the wittiest *hombre* in these parts. But you boys will be expected to work together, and I'd better take this opportunity to tell you — " He broke off when the sleepy-eyed hostler began to show an inordinate interest. The last thing he wanted was rumours flying around about the sort of characters Clem

157

Sanderson was hiring. He cleared his throat and finished: "I guess the rest will keep till we get home."

He rented a horse for Dobe Jenkins, and it developed that the tubby man's saddle and gear were lodged in the livery office, so that Eagen was forced to back-track on that score.

"Sorry for putting a burr under your tail, Dobie," he chuckled, patting the heavy shoulder.

"Forget it."

McLowry told them he expected to see another hand turning up soon, and while they waited he debated on the wisdom of hiring Nate Bream. In any case the ex-Split C rider might have changed his mind about going to work for Sanderson's Anvil.

In the meantime, Dobe Jenkins got acquainted with the grey horse from the stable, all the while lamenting the loss of his roan to Jack Keating. It was evident that Marty Eagen was being hard pressed to keep a halter on his barbed tongue, and McLowry could see he was bursting to make more fun at the stout man's expense.

He was about to give Nate Bream up as a lost cause when they heard a horse coming down the grey, otherwise quiet street. Its rider turned out to be the dark-complexioned cowhand who nodded coolly in McLowry's direction before letting his gaze absorb the other two.

"Glad to see you, Nate," McLowry greeted. "Meet Marty Eagen and Dobe Jenkins. Boys, this is Nate Bream, late of Split C. Which in no regard can be seen as a black mark against Bream. You still keen, Nate?"

The cowhand let a sudden grin dispel his wariness. "Sure thing, Frank. Looks like Anvil's going to have an outfit again. Hope you have a real good cook, though?"

"A cook?" McLowry grunted, somewhat put out.

"Yeah," Marty Eagen nudged with a twinkle in his eye. "Grub wrastler. Beans and bacon merchants, I always

159

call them. That's about as far as their culinary talents usually stretch."

"My, my!" Dobe Jenkins breathed in wonderment. "Did you get a load of that fancy lingo, Frank?"

"Never mind him, Dobe. He's just sporting his college education."

McLowry was serious despite the banter. He had joshed Jenny about putting a big pot on the stove, but he hadn't seriously considered whether she would be willing to wrangle chuck for a whole outfit.

Nate Bream's grin widened. "Fella, you don't even mean to say you've overlooked the most important item in a cowhand's life, next to warm socks?"

McLowry nodded ruefully. "I'll be damned," he said with feeling. "But we'll manage somehow. If you gents are willing to face hot lead from Marve Collins' bunch you shouldn't be all that pernickety about going hungry now and then."

"Mr McLowry, suh, I don't mind throwing lead at all," Marty Eagen retorted. "But having to eat it for breakfast or supper is a different thing entirely, and certainly not for this child."

The sally resulted in a gruff laugh from Nate Bream in which Dobe Jenkins was a hesitant participant. McLowry told them to be patient and see what happened.

They angled out on to the main street and sent their horses trotting through the dew-damp dust. Chimney pipes were beginning to spout woodsmoke like so many lazily stirring dragons. Swampers were busy with brooms and besoms. McLowry let his glance travel towards the Juarez cabin. Dobe Jenkins followed his gaze and spat from the side of his mouth.

"Mexican was killed there last night," he commented.

"I know," McLowry nodded. "Pedro Juarez. And his nephew is coming to work for us." He caught Nate Bream's frown. "You know Esteban Juarez, Nate?"

"Guess so. He worked for one of the homesteaders that Marve sent packing. Name of Alturo."

"You haven't got anything against Esteban then?"

"Hell no, Frank. Darkies and chinks and boys from manana land are all the one to me. They can all buy you a drink or plug you in the back, depending on their mood."

"Just like an American, huh?"

"Just like an American," Bream agreed. "So old Juarez cashed his chips? He was an odd sort of bozo."

"He was harmless," McLowry said in a tone that caused Bream to stare at him.

"Do you know something about the killing, Frank?"

"Maybe. I found him after he was shot. He left a message scrawled in his own blood. C-a-l."

"Calkin, by damn! Well, I'll be . . . But why did Deke want to kill the old Jasper?"

McLowry shrugged, his face drawn

in stern lines. "I happened to have just called on Pedro before he was shot. Esteban was there, too. The day I arrived in this territory Pedro followed me out to the graveyard, where I was looking for my brother's grave."

"Say, Frank, you're a stranger to these parts?" Dobe Jenkins queried in surprise. "And your brother was killed here? Then that's why — "

"It's why I'm here myself," McLowry admitted. "The reason I'm staying at Anvil. You might figure I'm just stringing Sanderson along until I find out who murdered Emmet, but there's more to it than that. I'd like to help Sanderson hold on to his outfit. In fact, I intend to see that he *does* hold on to it."

"Is that why you hired me too?" Nate Bream demanded hoarsely. "Maybe you thought I could tell you something about how Emmet McLowry was killed?"

"I never said that, Nate."

"Well, I don't know who killed your

brother, but I can tell you what I heard, for what it's worth."

"I'd admire to hear it, mister."

"They say that Marve was behind it."

"Well, thanks for that much. But I'll get to the bottom of it in my own time."

The town of Broken Horn lay behind them now; the huddled buildings were taking on shape and form as the sunlight glided roofs and flung long, ugly shadows. Marty Eagen pointed suddenly and called to McLowry and, sure enough, yonder was a horseman on their back-trail.

Nate Bream emitted a low whistle. "Sheriff Dan Bennet," he declared.

"Does that gent never sleep?"

"He's got a passing interest in me," McLowry explained with a dry chuckle. "Maybe he thinks I've started to find out things. I've a feeling he gets part of his pay from Marve Collins' hip pocket. Can anybody say that for a certainty?"

"Reckon nobody can," Nate Bream

replied. "But I've seen him and Marve go into the back room of that White Deer saloon more than once."

"Maybe they like a private game of checkers together," Marty Eagen suggested with tongue in cheek.

"Yeah, maybe you're right, Marty," McLowry acknowledged. "But you can't throw a brand on a man until you're dead sure who owns him . . . Anyhow, forget about the sheriff and let's burn some wind. It's quite a piece to Anvil Mesa."

★ ★ ★

Clem Sanderson was basking in the sunshine on the front porch of the ranch-house when the four horsemen rode through the gate and on to the tamped dirt of the front yard. At first sight of the newcomers Sanderson swung his rifle up, but when he recognized McLowry he gave vent to a whoop that brought Jenny from the house.

McLowry was not slow to detect the tide of colour that suffused the girl's cheeks as their eyes locked momentarily. She dipped her head in confusion while McLowry touched the brim of his hat.

"Hello again, Jenny."

"Frank! I'm so pleased to see you."

"Ahuh!" Marty Eagen drawled. "And what about the rest of us critters, Miss Sanderson? Ain't you glad to see us handsome fellas too?"

"Of course I am," the girl responded warmly and laughed. She came down the porch steps as they dismounted. Her eyes lifted to McLowry's once more, and on this occasion they were full of appreciation and gratitude.

"I'm pleased to see all of you." And she started in forthwith to shake hands with the arrivals, commencing with Dobe Jenkins.

McLowry introduced each man in turn. "Dobe Jenkins at your service, Jenny. The kid is called Marty Eagen, and maybe you've already met Nate

Bream, late of Split C?"

On the porch, Clem Sanders grunted something inaudible. McLowry looked at him and caught his breath at the fiery glance being directed at him.

"Do you and Bream know what you're about, Frank?" he asked anxiously.

"Guess so, Clem. Nate didn't like the way things were shaping at Collins' place and quit. I think he'll make a good hand."

Nate Bream held an alert poise until the rancher relented. Finally, Sanderson smiled and replied: "Anything you do has my blessing, Frank."

McLowry tipped Bream a sly wink. "Thanks, Boss," he said. "All right, boys, troop right up there and shake hands with Clem Sanderson. At the minute he's got a bad case of backache, but he'll get over it unless somebody shoots him off'n that bench, mistaking him for a crow maybe."

The three newly acquired hands mounted the steps and said hello to their employer. Jenny remained in the yard with McLowry, and her fingers came out to touch his own. He gripped her hand briefly while she whispered: "Mr McLowry, there's something simply wonderful about you."

"Truly?" He gave her a sidelong grin. "But you shouldn't say anything you might regret later, young lady. Many a mistake has been made in the heat of the minute."

"Truly," she returned softly. Her eyes sparkled and she started to say something else. But her red lips trembled and her small white teeth came down on the soft flesh. Then suddenly she wheeled up the steps and vanished into the house like a wraith. McLowry was nonplussed for a moment, but then he believed he understood why she had left him like that and he felt his spirits soar.

In the ensuing hour Frank McLowry was a prisoner in the grip of a heady glow. It was the same kind of feeling he got when he drank too much whisky or beer. The men took care of their horses, then washed and were shown to the bunkhouse by him. The newcomers displayed appreciation and satisfaction. Nate Bream followed McLowry outside and voiced a telling thought.

"I guess I can see why Marve has his eye on this place, Frank."

McLowry couldn't help countering mischievously: "Are you referring to Miss Jenny?"

"She would turn any man's head, mister. And that galoot Eagen has fallen, hook, line and sinker. But I'm talking about the outfit in general. It could be made to spin like a silver dollar."

"Clem would like to hear you say that, Nate." Part of McLowry's mind was dealing with what Bream had said about Marty Eagen. Marty was a handsome enough cuss when he thought about it. And there was no doubt that he had held on to Jenny's hand for longer than seemed necessary.

McLowry decided to push the dragon's

head out of sight and concentrate on making the men familiar with their surroundings. "I'll get Miss Jenny to help us get a clear picture of the whole of Anvil graze," he told them. "As you see, I've a lot to learn about this ranch myself."

"When do you reckon Miss Jenny will have the time?" Eagen put in with his inevitable grin. It was guileless and should have caused McLowry no concern, yet something about the blond youngster was beginning to grate on him, and he wondered if he hadn't made a mistake in hiring him.

"She'll have the time soon enough," he responded coolly. "And remember, sonny, you're here to work."

"Sure thing, Frank," the other crowed. "But you remember what I said about claims being staked."

"Far as I'm concerned, it still goes."

A swift retort sprang to McLowry's tongue but he choked it back. He was uncomfortably aware of Nate Bream and Dobe Jenkins watching him with some amusement. Worse still, he was aware also that his face must be as red as a sunset.

The rattling clamour of a wheel iron being beaten precluded further talk, and McLowry heaved a grateful sigh. "Appears somebody's been and rustled some chuck," he grunted. "And I don't know about you fellas, but I'm powerful hungry."

They ate at the long table in the ranch-house dining room. McLowry and Jenny had helped Clem Sanderson in from the porch and placed him at the head of the table. The food was good and plentiful, and was eaten for the most part in silence.

Afterwards they smoked, and Sanderson gave them a brief sketch of affairs as they stood at present. He outlined the troubled times that had 'brought Anvil to its knees,' as he put it.

"I was about to toss in my hand," he disclosed with a glance at McLowry. "But then Frank oozed along and perked me up. But I want to tell you boys that working here at the mesa won't be easy. It'll be hard. There could be bullets flying when Marve Collins hears what I've done. So, before we go any further, I'd like to give you men the chance to reconsider your — "

"No call for that, Mr Sanderson," Marty Eagen interjected. "We all know the score, and I guess fellas like us don't care much for the range being too quiet."

"Eagen's right," Dobe Jenkins contributed. "A bit of fighting'll keep me away from the card-sharps. I'm skinned as it is."

"Well, I'd just like to see Split C eat some crow," Nate Bream broke in flatly. "I'm with you, Sanderson, if you want to keep me."

McLowry puffed on one of his cigars, quiet, thoughtful. He decided he hadn't made such a bad start after all. Later, when the men left to sort out where they would sleep, he went into conference with Clem Sanderson. As soon as they were alone, the rancher hastened to compliment him.

"I like the looks of those three, Frank. I admit I got a surprise when you said Bream was a Split C ranny. But you know what you're about, and it does appear that Bream doesn't care much for Collins."

McLowry chose this juncture to tell Sanderson about the shooting of Pedro Juarez. He explained how Juarez had been generous in his friendship towards him. When McLowry explained that he believed the killer was Deke Calkin the rancher swore.

"I should have drilled him that day when I had the chance," he gritted.

"Maybe you'll get another chance, Clem. But I can't help feeling responsible for Pedro getting killed. I can't see Dan Bennet stirring far to hunt for the murderer."

"Dan Bennet's a bad case," Sanderson declared. "More's the pity."

McLowry told Sanderson about having offered a job to Juarez's nephew, and the rancher proved agreeable.

"I'd like to have about six good men to start off with, Frank. If Juarez comes it'll make five, and I've a hunch I'll be able to get around myself in another week or so."

"Don't rush things," McLowry advised. "Just keep toting your rifle on the porch, and holler when you see something that doesn't catch your fancy."

They talked for almost an hour, and at the end of that time McLowry had some idea about where he ought to start as ramrod of the outfit. Sanderson was anxious about the cattle that had wandered into the timber and brush. There was work there for a dozen men just now. A rough tally would have to be made in order to estimate the value of the stock on the hoof. Then the older stuff would be cut out and sold off to make way for the calf crop in the spring.

It was close to evening when Esteban rode up to the ranch-house and came under the muzzle of Clem Sanderson's rifle. His identity established, the Mexican went on to the bunkhouse where he found McLowry giving the crew a run-down on the nature of the work he proposed starting in the morning.

A glance told McLowry that Esteban had heard of Pedro's killing. He thought at first that the Mexican might change his mind about working for Anvil, but it turned out he was keener than ever to have a job.

Esteban had been to Broken Horn and had learnt of McLowry's arrangements with Oscar Dwire, the undertaker. He explained that he had given his approval and had spoken with the sheriff. It turned out that Esteban was far from happy with the reception Dan Bennet had given him.

"He said you had some idea about the killer," he told McLowry. "But he claimed you were jumping at straws and that you'd better watch your step. Señor McLowry," he added gravely,

"I believe they are planning how they can find an excuse to lock you up in jail."

"Let them try," McLowry responded with a hard grin. "Come and meet the boss, properly, pard. Then we can get down to business."

The rest of the day flew. By nightfall the four new hands had settled in and made themselves at home. McLowry knew that the welfare of any cattle outfit depended on how the riders felt about their boss and their quarters. He was sure they all shared a favourable impression and would give good value for the forty dollars a month they would earn.

After supper McLowry took a stroll in the deepening shadows, walking to a point where the mesa loomed starkly above him. It was dark now, a great hulking, black wall of rock that veered steeply into the star-spangled heavens. He found a deadfall and sank down to smoke one of his remaining cigars.

He was about to strike a match when he heard the low rustle of feet coming towards him. He flung the match aside and reached for the revolver at his hip.

"Frank . . . Are you there?"

He froze for an instant, hearing the quick thumping of his heart. Jenny called again, louder this time, before he answered.

"Over here."

Her slim form soon materialised from the darkness and he held her hand until she sank down beside him on the fallen tree.

"You've been keeping out of my way all day," she chided gently. "Is anything wrong, Frank?"

"Of course not. I've been pretty busy trying to break the new crew into some kind of shape — and that includes myself."

"Well, Marty Eagen seems able to find the time to talk to me. He came to the — "

"Eagen!" McLowry spat. "If that grinning, white-haired scallywag even dares to look in your direction I'll have his scalp. So help me!"

"You wouldn't?" Jenny laughed teasingly. "But whatever for, Frank? We've scarcely had enough time to say hello to each other. We certainly have a long way to go before we know each other at all . . . "

"Is that so?"

He was suddenly looming over her, dark, tall, fearsome. Something in his manner caused her to catch her breath sharply.

"Frank, please forgive me. I didn't mean to sound so brazen. I was just — joking, really."

"No, you weren't," he accused. "You were deliberately trying to make me mad. Jealous. I reckon. If you think that — "

"Frank, I . . . Really. I must be getting back to the house."

She rose and would have slipped under his arms had his hand not reached out and gripped her own. He spoke gently now, huskily.

"What's the hurry? Don't you want to talk, try to get to know each other better? I sure want to get to know you better, Jenny girl."

She fell against him then. She was scarcely any weight at all. But the effect of having her so close proved devastating to McLowry. Without really knowing what he was doing he cupped her face in his palms and covered her mouth with his own. And for what seemed an eternity, although it was really only fleeting seconds, the Anvil ranch and the mesa, and everything else except this girl in his arms, ceased to exist for Frank McLowry.

8

THEY had eaten breakfast and were ready to ride out as dawn trailed skirts of pearl and crimson across the eastern horizon. Jenny had been up and around first, starting the stove with billets that McLowry had chopped and stacked for her. She cooked for everybody.

Against McLowry's advice she insisted on going with them in order to make them familiar with the Anvil Mesa range. Sanderson had been muffled against the early chill and left on the porch with his rifle. Jenny endeavoured to impress on her father that there was no need for him to stand guard like that, but her advice fell on deaf ears. What would happen, Sanderson argued, if some of the Split C hardcases decided to take advantage of the ranch headquarters being deserted?

Nate Bream appeared preoccupied this morning and McLowry wondered if he was having a change of heart. One of the worst things that could happen to a man was hear his former friends brand him a renegade and, in relation to Marve Collins' outfit, this might result in drastic repercussions for Bream, Marty Eagen was as cocky and as cheerful as ever, and never missed a chance to poke fun at Dobe Jenkins. As far as Esteban Juarez was concerned, the Mexican was mostly still-faced and taciturn. But McLowry had no fears about Pedro's nephew not being able to give a good account of himself should the need arise.

Their tour commenced at the east flank of the awesome mesa and ran out in an irregular line that stretched for about ten miles into the west. Here was the south fork of the White River, and here, too, the boundary that divided Anvil and Split C.

They were angling southwards, away from the river fork, when McLowry picked up noise in a clump of willows on the far side of the offshoot. He wheeled to see two riders in the burgeoning sunlight, etched against the foliage like figures painted on a canvas. They made no move, but simply stared at Clem Sanderson's new crew.

McLowry noted how Nate Bream turned pale and mouthed a soft curse. Jenny had gone slightly pale as well and shot a worried look at McLowry. He merely dipped his head in understanding.

"They're just having a peek at us," he declared with a grin. "Some of Collins' boundary riders, Nate?"

"Couple of his toughs," Bream agreed. He spat forcefully. "Want to take the starch out of them and show them we ain't afraid of them?"

"Damn it, no!" McLowry barked. "Too nice a morning to start a range war."

"Frank's right," Jenny said, making an effort to assume command of the situation. "Let's ignore them. It isn't the first time I've caught them spying out the land. They think nothing of riding all over our grass."

"Because there was nobody to stop them," McLowry pointed out while his mood changed subtly. "But there's going to be a stop to it shortly."

A threshing of hooves in the undergrowth heralded the departure of the Split C men. They had twisted around and gone on into the thickets. Soon the morning quiet was reinstated. But there was a change in the air now. The tension and threat that would never be very far off became almost a tangible thing. McLowry felt it, and he knew that the others felt it. He let his gaze linger on Esteban Juarez for a few seconds, noticing how the Mexican's eyes glittered and how his mouth had become a thin, determined line in that dark, normally inscrutable face.

"Let's go," McLowry grunted and waited until Jenny moved out in front again.

They continued into the south,

riding steadily without pushing the horses unduly. At noon, with a fiery sun blazing overhead, they halted by a stream and ate a meal. All had recovered their high spirits, with the exception of Nate Bream, and McLowry felt obliged at length to take the man aside and speak quietly.

"Look, Nate, maybe this isn't the right neck of the woods for you. Those two *hombres* will hightail home to tell Marve you're riding with Anvil. Know what that means? Why not pull out altogether and find a range where you don't have to keep looking over your shoulder?"

The cowhand's brows knitted in a dark furrow. "You saying I might cause you more trouble than I'm worth?"

"Of course not. But I am thinking of some of your former pards laying up for you. Maybe that Deke Calkin. He must be a cold-blooded fiend."

"He's that right all right, Frank. So is Brin Eckols. But I'm not afraid of them."

McLowry shrugged, glancing to where the others were stretching out ahead. "Then that's fine, Nate. But don't risk your neck just to prove you're not afraid of your old outfit."

When they caught up, Marty Eagen was regaling Jenny with some story. The girl was laughing merrily, watching Eagen's features while he talked. McLowry's first instinctive reaction was a twinge of jealousy, but he soon stifled this when he remembered last night. He felt a quick thrill spread along his nerves as he studied the girl covertly, the way she had her hat tugged down so that her hair was trapped. But it wasn't quite imprisoned. Several strands escaped and blew in the soft breeze. Her tanned cheeks had taken on a rosy glow, and it was evident how she was enjoying this outing with men who would work for her, and protect her if needs be.

Riding along like that, McLowry let his thoughts run forward a little, to

185

the future and what it might hold for him. He had a notion that the time was coming when he would want to put down some roots. A man couldn't ramble around for ever like an aimless tumbleweed, a victim of every wind that blew. And wasn't Anvil Mesa as good a place as any to settle, always providing that he succeeded in finding Emmet's killer and that he survived whatever Marve Collins might decide to throw at him?

★ ★ ★

By two o'clock they were in a group of hills that backed off to a dark timberline. They had found cattle that wore the Anvil brand everywhere, and McLowry filed the locations away in his memory as Jenny talked and gestured and pointed.

They were making their way over the rim of a hollow when three horsemen appeared, cutting in on their left at a sharp angle. Nate Bream seemed to recognize them first and his reaction was startling. He uttered a hard curse and clawed for the gun at his hip, only to freeze at a crisp order from McLowry.

"Easy on, Nate. You'd better learn to control that itchy trigger-finger."

"But that's Collins and Brin Eckols," Bream choked. "They must have been following us."

"Leave it to me," was McLowry's curt response.

The three Split C men came on steadily and drew to a halt when they were level with the five from Anvil. McLowry spotted Marve Collins at once. He was in the centre, a tall man on a red stallion. He was dressed in good range garb and wore his wide-brimmed pearl grey hat at a jaunty angle. His tanned, handsome features relaxed in a wide smile while his icy blue eyes absorbed the group in a single glance. The blue eyes came to rest finally on Jenny.

"This is certainly a pleasure, Miss

Sanderson," Collins greeted in a strong, slightly husky voice. "And who are your friends?"

Jenny's cheeks had gone almost crimson during the initial moment of greeting, but she soon brought her feelings under control and met Collins' quizzical gaze coolly.

"This is my crew," she replied in a matter-of-fact manner and paused there, deciding she was under no obligation to elaborate.

"I see!" Once again the cold, bright eyes swept over the others, lingering longest on McLowry. For Frank's part, the blood raced in his veins. Here, he was sure, was the man who had ordered — if not actually carried out — the murder of his brother.

"I'll be doggoned," the man to the right of Marve Collins murmured. This one was short and powerfully built. He was dark and hawk-beaked, with a brash, predatory aura. His eyes were glued to Nate Bream as he spoke. "Funny the places rats go to when they leave a ship. Don't you reckon so, Boss?"

He had scarcely finished the sentence when Nate Bream's right hand drove for his six-shooter. McLowry caught the movement; caught, too, the way the stocky man's hand swept to his revolver. Nate's gun was clear of leather when McLowry's balled fist came in brutal contact with his wrist. The gun went flying while Bream swore luridly. The stocky, hawk-beaked individual whom McLowry had decided was Brin Eckols grinned at them from above his levelled Colt.

Eckols had no reason to imagine he had got the drop, however. Esteban and Marty Eagen had their respective weapons bared and pointed, so that Marve Collins snapped at Eckols to hold on.

Collins laughed uneasily and spread his hands to Jenny. "I apologise for Brin, Miss Sanderson," he chuckled. "But Nate there was always an impulsive person. Isn't that so, Nate?" And before Nate Bream had a chance to reply, Collins addressed McLowry. "Thanks anyhow, friend. That was quick thinking. There might have been a nasty accident if you hadn't butted in."

McLowry merely inclined his head curtly. He was watching the third member of the trio, a tall, skinny man who kept a cheroot trapped in the corner of his narrow mouth. This one had stayed back a little, his horse turned in such a way that he could ease his gun out without being immediately seen. His eyes collided with McLowry's flinty regard, and McLowry waited until the gun had been restored to its holster.

Frank had trouble curbing the anger that had begun swirling in him. Here was the opportunity to settle the score with Marve Collins and get the whole business over and done with. They were five three. And two of the trio comprised the driving force behind Split C. With Collins and Eckols out of the way, Emmet would be avenged and he could shed his Boothill brand. Of course he would have to lock horns with Sheriff Bennet afterwards, but he was confident that he could deal with Dan Bennet and that circuit judge.

Marve Collins had been speaking to Jenny without him really hearing what was said. McLowry realized that he was sweating and that a long shudder had run through him at the pictures he had been conjuring.

" . . . looks to me like you're putting on a show of strength, Jenny," Collins was saying to the girl.

Her slowness in answering gave McLowry the opportunity to cut in bleakly: "I figured you said we were still on Anvil land, ma'am? If that's the case, how come other folks can just ride where they please?"

Collins got the point, and his handsome features darkened with pulsating anger that boded ill for the tall man in front of him. Brin Eckols shifted his horse forward threateningly, but Collins gestured for him to back off. Then the Split C boss pointed a forefinger in the direction of Frank McLowry's nose.

"You get one simple fact through your high hat, mister," he grated, disposing of his bogus courtesy. "I ride where I please, and nobody's going to stop me. I don't know you, pilgrim, although I've got a hunch about you. But if you aim to stay around these parts, you'd better get yourself a rule book and read it."

"That's a mighty fine speech, Collins," McLowry drawled. "Yes, I think you've got a hunch about me right enough. You know who I am and why I'm in this neck of the woods. I'd been hoping to make your acquaintance soon, so I'm glad of the chance to issue due warning to anybody it applies to. If the man who murdered my brother Emmet takes his boots off at your place, he'd better make himself scarce. I intend to find him and make him pay in blood." His voice rose steadily in spite of his determination to remain cool. "And that means I don't give a hoot in hell who that killer happens to be. I'm going to get him and blow a hole through his guts you could drive a coach and four through."

"Hear the big man talk!" Brin Eckols cried scornfully. "Boss, you don't have to take that kind of guff from any of these saddle-tramps. Yeah, that's all they are, begging your pardon, Miss Sanderson," he appended with an evil grin. "Look at Bream there. Now what in blue blazes could you call a gent who — "

"Shut your yap," McLowry said thinly. "Miss Sanderson claims this is her land. Which means it's our land too, seeing as we're working for her. I'm her foreman, and I'm taking it on myself to speak for all of us. So I'm telling you gents right now to get the hell off this graze and don't come back unless you get an invite."

The brief silence that followed this speech vibrated with menace. Nate

Bream had recovered his revolver and pushed it away in its sheath, but he still looked mad enough to make another draw. Esteban and Marty Eagen were as stolid and as motionless as statues; they watched the three Split C men with unblinking vigilance. Jenny had drawn back a little and was staring at McLowry.

For McLowry's part, he was watching the changing expressions that flitted across Marve Collins' face. First, the boss of the Split C appeared on the brink of an eruption, but then he managed to gain control of his driving anger and mustered a small, cruel smile.

"I won't forget this, friend," he murmured to McLowry. "And I'm afraid you'll live to regret it."

"You won't live at all if you don't rattle your hocks," McLowry declared brutally. "That means now!"

For all he cared they could go for their guns right then and there and settle the matter in gunsmoke and hot lead, or they could tuck their tails in and live to take up the argument another day.

Marve Collins decided the issue. He whirled his horse about and sent it thundering towards his own territory. The other two dallied for about five seconds, obviously reluctant to back down. But they, too, knew when they were up against a man who meant every word he said. Brin Eckols gave a defiant yell as they hammered after their boss.

The three Split C men swept down the slope of the hollow and loped up the opposite side. They were outlined on the rim for a few minutes before dipping over and vanishing from sight. The drumming of their horses' hooves caused the air to throb and pulsate, but then the sounds diminished, and eventually ceased altogether.

Marty Eagen broke the tension with a high, ready laugh. "So that's a sample of what we're up against?" he crowed. "Well, Frank, all I can say is we should have stamped on them when we had them where we wanted them."

"Damn right," Nate Bream growled. He was dark-browed, trembling with what McLowry interpreted as suppressed fury at having to put up with Eckols' haranguing. Dobe Jenkins and Esteban remained calm and unflustered.

"Seems to me you're a gent to ride the river with, Mr McLowry," Jenkins observed with a topsided grin. "That hellion figured he'd bluff you to the limit and then ride over you. It took something to make Marve Collins fall back in his tracks."

"Don't bank on him staying there, Dobe," McLowry counselled while he elbowed moisture from the sweatband of his hat. "Collins is smarter than a sackful of foxes. I got a good chance to figure him then. I admit I was thinking of my brother, and I was sorely tempted to shoot his teeth down his throat. But we've got to remember that it's a cow outfit we're running and not a school for gunmen."

He glanced at Jenny and saw she was pale and subdued, busy with her thoughts. She was worried, of course, he knew, and perhaps he could have spared her that ugly scene. But Marve Collins just had to be brought up short sooner or later.

McLowry knew, too, that events had taken a definite twist for the worse. Heretofore, Collins' outfit had more or less tolerated Anvil, mostly for the fact that Clem Sanderson had been rendered toothless; but the complexion of things had altered. Anvil had girded its loins and was primed for battle. It was to be expected then that the Split C boss would act accordingly, with no holds barred.

Marty Eagen suggested trailing Collins and his companions to make certain they crossed back into their own territory, and to McLowry's surprise Nate Bream proved to be of a similar mind. But Frank shook his head. The hand had been played, and it must be left to Collins to deal the next cards.

"You'll have your fill of fighting shortly," he added on a grimmer note. "Right now we want to find out more about the land we're fighting for. Are you able to continue, Jenny?"

"Of course I am, Frank. Shall we go?"

★ ★ ★

It was sundown when they came in sight of the ranch buildings again. Riding into the front yard, Jenny's gaze immediately lifted to the porch where they had left her father. Sanderson was not on his accustomed bench and the girl was thrown into panic.

"Dad!" she cried, bringing her horse to a skidding halt. "Dad . . . where are you?"

McLowry took the porch steps in a couple of leaps and thrust on through to the living room. "Sanderson!"

"I'm here. What's all the fuss about?"

They found him in the kitchen,

drinking a mug of coffee by the stove. He put a beaming smile on them that McLowry and the girl found puzzling. They exchanged quizzical looks.

"Seems to me you might have found a gold mine, old-timer. What about letting everybody in on the secret?"

"It's pure gold right enough, Frank. Listen, folks, I made it in here on my own. Haven't you noticed? Figured I might starve if I had to stay out there all day." He stood up and demonstrated how he could take a few steps, shakily admittedly, but it was the first real sign that he was making a comeback.

Jenny hugged him, crying a little as she did so. Sanderson patted her head while his faded eyes lifted to McLowry.

"Well, how did it go? You look sort of ruffled, Frank. Say, you didn't run into any of that Split C crowd?"

McLowry told Sanderson of their encounter with Marve Collins and his two men. While he talked, Jenny laid her fingers on his arm, her gaze absorbing him.

"Oh, Dad, Frank was wonderful," she exclaimed when she could no longer contain herself. "He told them to get off our land. You should have seen Marve's face! He was ready to explode right then and there. Eckols looked as if he was having to swallow poison . . . "

"Well, I like the sound of that," Sanderson chuckled. Then, soberly: "Was Nate Bream there?"

"Sure he was. Nate wanted to use his gun, and it was a job just keeping him calm."

"Well, well! So Anvil has stood up to Split C at last? But we mustn't go off at half cock, Frank. You know what this will mean now?"

"I know well enough. We knew what it would mean before we started, didn't we? But I reckon we're ready to pitch back anything they throw at us."

"That's good, boy. That's just about the sweetest music I've heard in many a long day . . . "

★ ★ ★

In another week Clem Sanderson was able to get around under his own steam. During that time McLowry kept his crew hard at work. Cattle were hazed out of the timber and brush, out of the many canyons they had decided to locate in, and brushy brakes and treacherous swampland. All in all, it was a highly rewarding time for Frank McLowry. Quite apart from his original motive for taking a job with Anvil, he found that the task of putting the ranch back on its feet brought a satisfaction he had not even dreamed of.

The men had to work with one eye on the task at hand and the other on the look-out for danger from Split C riders. But as the days passed it appeared that Marve Collins had given up the idea of acquiring Anvil, or it might be that he was merely biding his time until the signs were right to make his move.

Trouble struck half-way through the second week, confirming McLowry's fears that Collins had merely been treading water. Marty Eagen and Esteban were ambushed out near the timberline. They managed to beat off the three attackers who opened fire on them, but Marty's horse was shot from under him, and it required all of McLowry's persuasive powers to keep the cowhand from heading directly to Split C and forcing a showdown.

That night another conference was called in Clem Sanderson's office at which all of the crew members were present.

"This is Collins' first blow since Frank took over," the rancher told them. "I read it as a sign of more trouble to come, and *pronto*. Esteban, you and Marty there have sampled what that outfit can get up to. I wouldn't hold a man who wants to keep his hide in one piece. That's why I'm giving you all another chance to get out if you want to."

McLowry was only slightly surprised when Eagen erupted in a stream of profanity. Frank was of the opinion that, while Sanderson's remark could be called reasonable, it was unfair in that it carried an implication which could not be mistaken. Therefore, he decided he ought to butt in.

He told Sanderson bluntly: "Clem, I believe I'm saying what we all think. None of us is going to run away from Split C. Figure it out for yourself. Dobe here has a grudge against a joker called Luke Keating who also wears a Split C brand. Esteban has it in for Deke Calkin. Whatever ideas Sheriff Bennet might have about the killing of old Pedro, Esteban and I are sure that Calkin was the gunman. Now Marty has a good reason for wolf-howling Collins. Nate would like the opportunity to spit in Marve's eye. So what more do you want to hear?"

At this Clem Sanderson shrugged and grinned. "All right, gents, I promise to say nothing more on that particular subject. But, Frank, I'm going to get you to saddle a nag for me tomorrow. I'm fit enough to hit the trail, and if there's going to be all the fun and games you fellas hint at, then I reckon I'm entitled to my share."

★ ★ ★

He did manage to get aboard his big chestnut horse the next morning. McLowry and Jenny advised him to stay close to headquarters for a day or so, which he did. In the meantime, slowly but surely, Anvil's new crew was getting a beef herd together. Nearly all of the men reported seeing drifting riders from time to time. In spite of the warning McLowry had issued to Collins about staying on the right side of his fence, Split C men continued to cross over at the river fork to spy on what was going on.

The herd was ready to take the trail to the Broken Horn stockyards on the following Friday. McLowry had carried letters from the post office in town, and Sanderson announced he had a buyer waiting for delivery. On the short visits he made to Broken Horn, McLowry knew he was under the eye of Sheriff Dan Bennet; for all that, however, the lawman made no move to approach him.

Early Saturday morning, fifteen hundred head of three- and four-year-old steers went over the river and began the trek to Broken Horn. Sanderson, against his daughter's wishes, went along with the drovers. Esteban and Jenny remained at the ranch, with Esteban under orders to keep a sharp look-out.

It was noon when the cowhands reached town and pushed the cattle towards the holding pens. The buyer's agent was there to make a tally on the stuff passing through the gate. Afterwards, a cheque was passed over and the buyer's agent was invited to have a drink in one of the saloons. This formality dispensed with, McLowry cut out for a barber shop where he had a shave, hair trim and a hot bath.

Sanderson told his men they could

spend a couple of hours in town before riding back to the ranch. If McLowry had his way he would have ordered the boys back at once. After all, Jenny and Esteban were on their own out there, at the mercy of Collins' hardcases should they decide to perpetrate more mischief.

At six o'clock they all met up in the hotel and had a first-class meal paid for by their boss. The rancher was in high spirits over the transaction he had made, and he enjoyed being back in the saddle. McLowry, therefore, was reluctant to introduce any hint of anxiety.

"It's getting like old times again, Frank," Sanderson remarked as he distributed a handful of cigars. "If we can keep Split C out of our hair for long enough, Anvil will soon be a spread to reckon with."

Sanderson would have lingered on, talking and drinking, growing more expansive. But finally, McLowry decided that enough was enough. They were heading along the street when he missed Dobe Jenkins, and when he asked Marty Eagen about the rider he learned that Dobe had slipped off while they were talking in the hotel.

"What in hell for?" McLowry grumbled peevishly. "Look, you fellas go on to the livery and get the nags ready for home. I'll hunt up Dobe and join you there."

It turned out that there was no trace of Jenkins on the main street, and McLowry really grew angry. Sanderson had given them all some money that would be deducted from their pay, and it was possible that Dobe had surrendered to a yen for a poker game.

He managed to run the cowhand to earth at last in the Sage Saloon.

Dobe was turning from the bar where an empty glass stood when McLowry spoke his name sharply. The tubby man was red of face and bright of eye, bad signs in McLowry's book. He grinned cheekily and gave his foreman a thumbs-up signal.

"Be with you shortly, Frank. Just spotted a joker I want to speak to."

McLowry chewed back a protest and held on at the bar. He watched Dobe head for a table where four men were playing cards and saw Dobe tap a shaggy-headed character on the shoulder.

When the man turned his face it permitted McLowry a glimpse of a rough-hewn profile and thick, beetling brows. He glanced up at Dobe and laughed.

"Hey, if it ain't Mr Jenkins again! Well, well! Here, sit down, Fat Boy, and take a hand."

"Not this trip, Keating," Dobe informed him in a voice that carried over the room. "I just spotted you and I thought I'd get something off my chest."

McLowry frowned and pulled a slow breath through his teeth. He didn't like this situation one little bit. It was obvious now that Dobe was three-quarters drunk, and he should have hauled him out of the saloon in the first instance.

The shaggy-headed character gave another of his spine-scraping laughs and poked a finger at the cowhand. "Oh, yeah, I nearly forgot, Fatty. You're working for the Sanderson outfit, I believe. Is that what you hanker to get off your chest? Well, rumours have a habit of travelling and a little bird brought me this one."

"Well, you just get ready for another little bird to happen by, Keating. That roan you won off'n me . . . it wasn't a fair game at all."

Jenkins might as well have cracked a whip above the table. All four men gathered around it peered up at him. Then curious eyes leaped to see how the shaggy-headed Keating would react. The big fellow winked broadly at his companions, cleared his throat loudly, heaved his chair back. Standing, he dwarfed Dobe Jenkins by a foot. His shoulders were wide and square. His great arms hung at his sides like overgrown tree branches.

"Now, Mr Jenkins, sir," he began in a purring tone. "I reckon you'd better come a mite closer so I can hear you right. For a minute then I figured you said I hadn't played fair. Say," he went on with a hard chuckle, "maybe that air out at Anvil Mesa has done something to your brain . . . "

"You bet it has," Jenkins flung back. He appeared totally fearless, completely unabashed. "Cleared my brain for a start. I want my roan back, Keating, like I said, I ain't going to pay for another horse when I own one already that was took away from me by a skunk tinhorn."

Keating threw his great head back and laughed heartily. But then his demeanour underwent a change that should have warned Jenkins. He pushed his thick finger into the tubby man's chest.

"Fatty," he said with mock gravity, "you're just about to be struck by a terrible sickness. Don't that bother you none? Wouldn't you rather shut your big mouth and crawl into a corner until you sober up? If you do I promise I'll hold my hand until you can see straight and talk straight. So what about it, fella? You know it ain't polite to go around calling folks fancy names."

"I got a hell of a lot of good names that fit you, Keating," Jenkins snarled as he fell back a step. "What about cheat? What about card-sharp, you son of a bitch?"

"Dobe!" McLowry called hoarsely.

"You stay out of this, Frank."

"Yeah, you stay out of this, Frank," Keating mimicked without looking in McLowry's direction. "This is strictly between me and Fat Boy here. Now, Mr Jenkins, everybody is listening to what you're saying. And all these folks can sure hear what I'm saying. I'm saying I don't want to hurt you, mister. Know what I mean? So why don't you just back up and shut up?"

"When I get my roan horse back, you louse!"

"You're going to get a piece of lead in your fat belly, mister — *Now!*"

"Hold it!" McLowry yelled, his hand dipping for his Colt as Keating's fingers drove for his holstered six-gun.

9

LUKE KEATING swivelled on his toes, then froze, momentarily paralysed by McLowry's piercing call. His eyes found the speaker and immediately flared with a new venom, McLowry's fingers were splayed above his gun butt, taloned in eager readiness.

Dobe Jenkins mouthed a curse. "Why couldn't you keep out of this, Frank?"

"Because you've signed up with Anvil, mister. That makes you Anvil property until you want to collect your time — or get yourself killed for acting the fool."

"And that won't be long," shaggy-headed Keating scowled, "unless you drag him out of here, *hombre*."

At a stroke the gambler and roughneck had adopted the role of someone wrongfully accused of a misdemeanour.

But he didn't fool McLowry, and Keating knew that quite well. McLowry had immediately labelled the man as deadly as poison and as treacherous as a sidewinder.

Keating relaxed somewhat, poked his finger at Dobe Jenkins. "And let me give you a word of advice, friend, before our ways part," he said smoothly. "If you aim to call somebody a card-sharp you'd better make sure you've a sober head on your shoulders."

"I'm calling you that now," Jenkins retorted recklessly. It seemed that, for good or ill, Dobe was determined to force the issue.

Luke Keating glanced at McLowry with darkening features before studying the fat man in front of him. Somebody sniggered at the back of the room. McLowry felt caught between two fires now; he was tempted to let the pig-headed Jenkins fend for himself. He was furious with him just then.

"Know something, Fat Boy," Keating grated in a low-pitched tone, "I'm going to bore you — *right now!*"

McLowry moved swiftly, but the move was towards Dobe Jenkins rather than Luke Keating. Before Dobe could grasp his intention McLowry had whipped his gun away from him. Dobe cursed and swung his fist at McLowry's head, and McLowry flung the punch wide before sending his bunched knuckles slamming at Dobe's jawline.

It was a heavy, well-timed blow, and resulted in the fat man flailing around in a circle before sliding down in a graceless heap.

McLowry had a faint grin at his mouth as he raised his head to the tight-featured Keating. "He's my rider, so anything you have to say to him you can say to me."

"I was going to bore him, friend," the big man declared with contempt thickening his voice. "You wouldn't like me to take *that* out on you?"

"It's your play," McLowry told him, his grin taking on a perceptible chill.

"But I might as well tell you that I think Dobe was right."

"About calling me a card-sharp?" Keating demanded in hoarse disbelief. A change ran through his demeanour; his eyes sparkled dangerously. His right hand contrived an arch at his side.

"You've got it the right way up, mister," McLowry assured him.

It was the moment Dobe Jenkins chose to stir on the floor. He gripped the edge of the counter and tried to haul himself to his feet. Upright, he leaned back against the bar, rubbing his bruised jaw and considering, first Keating and then McLowry. A throbbing silence gripped the saloon. Luke Keating had begun to sweat and the perspiration pasted a bright sheen on his forehead. His gun had quivered in anticipation of a signal from his tortured brain. Draw and kill this stranger with the mocking voice and the contemptuous eye, the message said. *Draw and be killed by him*. Which would it be? A man should never have to make such a damnable decision.

A shudder ran through the big fellow. He burst out laughing in a manner that was supposed to infect everyone else so that they would relax and see that he was just joking after all and that he really had no intention of killing Dobe Jenkins or the tall stranger who had taken up the cudgel on Dobe's behalf. The laugh became strained, heavy with the weight of reluctant submission. Keating could scarcely recognize the coward's streak he suddenly found in himself, much less acknowledge its existence.

His voice was a dry rasp as he said: "I haven't got any fight with you, mister. Anyhow, I was just funning with the fat man."

"You're a liar, Keating," McLowry retorted flatly. "You just ran short on nerve. So I want you out of this saloon *pronto*."

"Say, you listen here . . . "

"No, *you* listen, sonny. Get out of here. And the next time you have a yen to pull your gun on an Anvil man, think of me. Because I'll come after you and settle the score — just as I aim to settle the score for the killing of Emmet McLowry. Go on — scat!"

And that was how Luke Keating went. Like a sour-tempered, ragged-haired old alley cat that had met its match. The Split C man shouldered through the batwings and disappeared into the mellowness of the evening. No sooner had he gone than a buzz of talk erupted, as if a cloud of bees had invaded the saloon.

Dobe Jenkins looked sheepish. "I'm sorry, Frank. I just figured I had to call him out."

"Forget it. Time we were hitting the trail."

McLowry preceded Dobe into the street, glancing quickly around him as soon as he cleared the saloon doorway. Even so, he was almost taken by surprise as someone yelled his name from the middle of the roadway. At the same time a revolver thundered and a bullet snarled past McLowry's left ear to bury itself in one of the red batwing doors.

Then McLowry was heaving Dobe Jenkins aside and clawing his six-shooter clear at the same time. Keating triggered his second shot on the instant McLowry's Colt belched flame and smoke.

The shaggy-headed man appeared to break in the middle like a doll with the sawdust stuffing torn from it. He fell to his knees, flopped on one elbow, screamed an oath and contrived to lever his arm to fire another shot. McLowry's gun drummed twice more in rapid succession and the Split C man pitched forward into the dust.

It was a signal for everybody to commence shouting at once, to start running towards the scene of the shooting. Heavy boots thumped along the boardwalks and scraped to a halt. A couple of women with baskets who had been about to emerge from a store ducked back inside. Dobe Jenkins was cold sober now as he righted himself. He looked pale and frightened.

"What the hell have you done . . . ?"

"Only what was necessary . . . "

"Then we'd better get out of here, mister. I see the law moseying this way."

It was true. Sheriff Dan Bennet was stalking towards them. Deputy Jed Deakin dogging his steps. Bennet stabbed a hard look at McLowry before angling over to stand above the body of Luke Keating. He stooped and made a hurried examination, then closed with McLowry.

"He's dead," he declared incredulously. "You shot him?"

"He tried to drill me as soon as I hit the street," McLowry told him. "There are plenty of witnesses around to bear me out."

"One of Marve Collins' boys," Bennet said through his teeth. "So the pot's beginning to boil over? And if this is the start of a vendetta, mister, I'm going to stop it right here."

"There's not a damn thing you can do about it," McLowry informed him coldly. "But maybe there is. You might ride out and see Marve Collins. Tell him what happened. Tell him he'd better call his thugs to heel. And when you're at it, maybe you should tell him to hand over the gent who killed my brother."

Jed Deakin was moving in menacingly when Bennet raised an arm to stop him. "Never mind, Jed. This'll work itself out without our help."

"I'm glad you see it that way," McLowry applauded sarcastically. He straightened his hat, slapped the palms of his hands together. "Come on Dobe. We'd better light out for home."

When they joined Sanderson and the others at the livery stable it developed that news of the fracas had just percolated that far. Sanderson was for having it out with Dan Bennet before he left town, but McLowry persuaded him to let the matter rest where it was.

"Sheriff reckons I've lit the fuse that'll send your outfit sky-high without any help from him," he added bitterly. "And maybe that's just what I've done, Clem."

"Better now than later," the rancher rejoined philosophically. "You've done what I've wanted to do for a long time, Frank. All right, fellas, let's hit the trail."

★ ★ ★

Starlight was rampant in the heavens by the time they crossed the river and rode along the cottonwood avenue to gain the ranch yard. Clem Sanderson rode out in front, and when he drew up at the front of the house he panted a hard curse.

"There's something wrong. There's nobody here!"

The initial shock was like a hard blow to the pit of McLowry's stomach. His heart skipped a beat, then began hammering wildly. Jenny, he thought frantically. Nothing must happen to Jenny. But nothing could have happened to her . . .

There was no light anywhere in the house: that was certain. And he knew as well as the others that, if Jenny were about, she would have shown herself immediately.

He and Clem Sanderson were first to clamber from their saddles. Sanderson stumbled and almost fell, so that McLowry was obliged to support him. Then McLowry left the old man and scrambled up the porch steps. The door opened to a push and he hurried on inside, calling Jenny's name while he scratched a match aflame for the ceiling lamp in the kitchen.

The stove was cold — a bad sign. The coffee pot was equally cold. There was the smell of desertion, a sense of some strong presence having been withdrawn. Without the girl this place would be no more than a hollow shell.

"That damned Esteban," he grumbled illogically.

"Where in blazes could they be, Frank?"

"Hell, how do I know?"

He brushed past Sanderson and returned to the yard. The men remained standing by their horses, dim figures in the star-dappled shadows. "Hold it," he told them. "Jenny's not here, Esteban neither. I'm going to see what horses are missing."

He groped around in the musty darkness of the barn until he found the lantern and got it burning. Clem Sanderson bustled in, limping a little, groaning in despair.

"Frank, you don't figure that Mex would — "

"Take it easy, Clem. Esteban's horse has gone. So has the grey."

"That means they've lit out somewhere. But where, Frank? I'll go crazy if anything has happened to my girl."

"You stay here," McLowry told him. "I'll take Marty and scout around. They can't be far away."

"No . . . I'm going with you. And

don't try stopping me."

"That settles it then," McLowry decided. "We'll all go. But we'll have to switch horses."

In a short time they were freshly mounted and riding back through the cottonwoods. At this juncture McLowry was dry-mouthed, grim, edgy. If Esteban had snaked on them he would suffer for it. But somehow, he couldn't see the Mexican doing anything that would hurt the girl or her father. But something must have happened to take them away from the ranch-house. The question was what?

They rode for an hour without any definite aim, drifting across the moon-silvered grasslands like wraiths. Far ahead of them loomed the raw upheaval of cliffs, the tortuous canyons and deep ravines. Beyond that lay the trail leading to Broken Horn.

McLowry had a sudden inspiration. "Swing north-west," he cried. "Over the river."

"Split C!" Clem Sanderson exclaimed.

225

"But they wouldn't — "

"You don't know, damn it. They might."

They switched course at once, veering off to the west now. The sky was fiery with stars. A pungent breeze sifted down from the cliffs on their right. Anvil Mesa loomed over everything like a huge, sprawling monstrosity, as if engraving its permanence on a scene that was at best ephemeral. The horses snorted and blew, harness jingled, leather pulled and creaked.

They were still two miles from the White River when they came on the loose horse.

The beast pranced away when they tried to get close to it, and McLowry went after it. He finally cornered the loose mount and brought it back to the others.

"Who's is it?" Clem Sanderson croaked.

"Esteban's. With all the gear on. It's cool enough, so it hasn't been running."

"But where is he, Frank? Where's Jenny?"

"Don't worry, old-timer, we'll find them." He told Marty Eagen to look after the mount. "Keep going for the river. I've a hunch we're on the right track."

Try as he did to sound optimistic, McLowry felt as if a cloud were setting over him. If Esteban had become separated from his horse it pointed to a single, dire conclusion: he must be lying somewhere, badly hurt or dead.

He told the others to spread out and make a close search. He was pulling away when Dobe Jenkins reined in beside him. "You don't reckon he's dead, Frank?"

"Hard to say, Dobe. But we're going to find out."

"The girl," Jenkins said thickly. "What could have happened to her?"

McLowry started to frame a reply, but his tongue clove to the roof of his mouth. There were some things that didn't bear thinking about.

They were close enough to the river to hear its dull roar when a feeble shout came from the direction of a hollow. McLowry swung his horse over the rim and entered the swelling shadows cautiously, eyes darting this way and that, hand resting on his gun butt. The others hammered after him and then broke apart, trying to pinpoint the location of the call.

It was Nate Bream who came on Esteban. The Mexican was alive, but only just. He muttered and moaned, writhing with the pain that gripped him.

"Where are you hurt, pard?"

McLowry soon made out the bloodied wounds, in the chest and stomach. It was a miracle that Esteban was still alive. A whisky flask was produced from Sanderson's saddle kit and McLowry uncorked it and held it to the Mexican's lips.

"Can you tell me what happened, pard?"

"Calkin," Esteban whispered. "Two others. They must have seen you leave . . . They crept up on the house. Hit me on the head. I heard the señorita scream. They rode away and I followed. They . . . fired at me and I fell from my horse."

"Well, don't you worry none. We're going to get you on a nag and take you home. We'll soon fix — " He broke off as Esteban's head suddenly fell back, and he knew he was dead.

McLowry stooped there for a long time, aware of a poisonous fury running in his veins. He looked up at the white faces gathered about and released a long sigh.

"Wish I'd let him be where he was," he groaned. "I just made it easier for that Collins snake to kill him."

"Don't say that, Frank." Clem Sanderson placed a hand on his shoulder. "If anybody's to blame it's me."

"There's just one sidewinder to blame," Marty Eagen cut in vehemently.

"And we all know who it is."

"Deke Calkin," McLowry murmured. He winced as Sanderson's fingers dug in. "Yeah, I know what you're thinking, Clem. Jenny. It seems they grabbed her at the house and took her away."

"My girl! What have they done with my girl?"

"They won't harm her for sure. Even Collins knows he wouldn't get away with that . . . All right, men, first things first. Get Esteban's saddle blanket."

The body was rolled in the blanket and secured to the loose horse. Sanderson suggested leaving the horse hobbled until they came back, but McLowry recommended starting it out for home. They would see to it that a proper funeral was arranged. They watched the horse gallop away after it had been given a hard slap on the rump to get it going.

The shadow of death hung over the small group as it set off once more, and added to that was the grim possibility that something serious had befallen

Sanderson's daughter. They reached the river and crossed at the ford, and here Nate Bream moved into the lead, guiding them across land with which he was thoroughly familiar.

The breeze freshened, rustling the trees and brush along the way, playing coolly on their set faces. Clem Sanderson had lapsed into a frozen silence, and when McLowry drew alongside him and spoke, he received only a preoccupied grunt in reply.

McLowry wondered if the rancher was regretting the whole business now, if he wished he had never met Emmet's brother. McLowry wondered if he didn't regret riding to Anvil Mesa himself. But how could he have hoped to settle the score for Emmet if he hadn't visited Anvil?

They were moving through grass country now, and had breasted a hill where the moonlight picked them up in stark relief when a horse shifted towards them out of the shadows, a Split C night-hawk, likely.

"Who is it?" came a rasping demand.

"Anvil," McLowry answered clearly, levelling his six-gun on the man. "And don't try to stop us visiting, friend."

"But that's a crazy idea! You can't — "

"Haul off," Clem Sanderson warned the lanky man. "Or maybe you'd rather take what's coming to you."

"Is that Mr Sanderson?" the man croaked in disbelief.

"Nobody else. Now buzz."

A grim smile played at McLowry's mouth as he watched the night-hawk pull his mount away to the side and ride off. And just as he was congratulating himself on getting past the night guard so easily, the man suddenly spun in his saddle with his revolver bellowing.

Crimson flame spewed across the distance separating them, and no sooner had the drumming echo died than Clem Sanderson was triggering furiously. The Split C man screamed and flung himself across the neck of his bolting horse. But Sanderson had no intention of letting him get away now. He took aim and fired once more, and the night-hawk toppled sideways from his saddle and spilled into a well of darkness.

McLowry's heart trip-hammered against his ribs. "That'll waken the whole damn range," he snarled at Sanderson.

"There was no other way, damn it. He was set on killing us if he could."

"Nate," McLowry called to Bream, "are we far out from Split C headquarters?"

"Not so far. There's a timber windbreak up ahead. The layout's on the other side."

Marty Eagen had angled off to examine the fallen rider. He clambered back into his saddle and rejoined the others. "He's dead, Boss."

"A good way for him to be, Marty," Sanderson rasped. "There'll be a lot more cold meat before I'm through with this crowd," he added with a quick look at McLowry.

McLowry groaned inwardly. Old Clem could get out of hand just when they needed cool heads and steady nerves. He might spoil everything and frustrate their efforts to discover what had happened to Jenny. In the meantime, Nate Bream forged ahead, making for the thick wall of timber that resembled the outer barricade of a fortress.

Another half-hour passed and they broke out of the trees to see the lights of the Split C headquarters far down in a hollow below them. They grouped together at a word from McLowry.

"This has got to be handled the right way," he impressed on them while fixing his gaze steadily on Clem Sanderson. "Anybody who goes off at half-cock will feel the barrel of my gun across his skull. I'm sorry, Clem, but that includes you as well."

Sanderson started to retort, then changed his mind and inclined his head. "Whatever you say, Frank. Reckon they heard the shooting?"

"Wind's coming at us. Let's hope they didn't. All right, gents, let's open the ball."

They filed into the hollow, spreading out a little at a signal from McLowry. While striving to maintain a steady nerve, he could feel icy fingers clawing at his vitals, working savagely there. He knew it was concern for the girl. If anything happened to Jenny on account of his actions he would never forgive himself.

The dimly-lit windows of the main house were in view when hoofbeats set up a hollow thunder in the darkness. Horsemen were on the move, coming in their direction. Three at least, McLowry calculated.

"Play it cool," he hissed. "Let me handle it."

The horsemen came on, slowed when they were able to distinguish the shadowy forms of the Anvil men. There were three in the group, as McLowry had judged. The tip of a cigarette glowed like a firefly, then arched away as it was flicked out of reach.

"Who goes there? Jeb . . . it ain't you and your pals?"

"Come and see," McLowry invited brashly.

A lot of whispering broke out then. The Collins men parted, contriving a loose circle. They would have their guns out by now, McLowry knew, and they might be under orders to use them without asking too many questions.

Sweat moistened Frank's jaw, salted his lips. He watched carefully as the three began to close the circle. Then one of them detached himself and came forward boldly. "Well, well!" he chuckled. "I got a smell in my nose says this might be Anvil come to drink tea with the boss . . . Am I right there, boys?"

"You're right as rain, Calkin," McLowry drawled. "Where's the big man himself at?"

"Ain't very far away. Say, is that Sanderson himself, I see?"

"It's me," the rancher replied. "I want to see your boss, Deke."

"At this hour? Sorry, gents, but it's too late in the day for tea. We're just heading out to do our spell of night-hawking."

"That's something you're pretty good at, ain't it?" Sanderson observed. "But we're here to see Collins, and we're not moving until we do."

"Hear that, fellas?" the cowhand chuckled. "Pretty big talk for a small man, ain't it now?" His voice hardened. "You'd better remember something, Mr Sanderson, sir: you're a purty long way from home. Sort of out of your depth, you might say."

"Not that far, Calkin. We're heading on to the house, and you're not stopping us."

"He's right," McLowry chipped in brusquely. He touched the butt of his Colt. "Get out of the way, mister. We intend to see your boss. We found Esteban and he was able to tell us a couple of things before he cashed."

Calkin's gasp was a little choking sound. He appeared to crouch over his saddle. McLowry let his eyes shift briefly to the pair at Calkin's back. Would Calkin risk taking on the five Anvil guns?

"I don't know what you're talking about," Calkin blustered. "We know nothing about your Mex."

"You know plenty, mister," McLowry said. "And you'd better cough up as well about where Sanderson's girl is."

The cowhand's laugh was a raw, explosive braying that grated on McLowry's nerves. His fingers itched to haul out his gun and put a bullet in the man's black heart.

"You've got him, Frank," Clem Sanderson said at McLowry's side. "Jenny must be down there somewhere."

"Hold on!" Calkin erupted. "I don't know what you're all gabbing about. But it doesn't matter a damn anyhow because you ain't getting any closer to the house."

"Have you got the guts to stop us?" McLowry pealed at him. "You're covered, you fool! Start shooting and it's going to be the bloodiest party you ever heard of. Only you won't be alive, Deke, to clean up the mess."

For the space of ten seconds there was a deathly silence. Then Calkin backed his horse off slowly, and McLowry knew that treachery was afoot. The wonder was that no one else down yonder at the ranch buildings had been alerted by the commotion.

"All right," Calkin said with a weak laugh. "I guess there's no reason why we can't talk this over quiet and sensible . . . "

"Get my daughter, you bastard," Clem Sanderson yelled furiously. "I'm damned if I'm going to sit here and dicker with you rats — "

Calkin's revolver barked before the rancher could finish, and then McLowry's Colt was bucking against the palm of his hand to the deadly song of flying bullets.

McLowry made sure that his first slug cut Deke Calkin from the saddle of his horse, and Deke fell like a sheaf of corn falling before a reaper's scythe.

10

IT seemed that all hell broke loose after that. Bullet-tipped spume lashed hither and thither. McLowry's cheek was scorched. A slug speared past his left shoulder. The exchange of gunfire appeared to go on for ever, but in reality the whole thing was over in thirty pulsating seconds.

Two of the Split C men were dead and the other one was charging back down the slope to the ranch buildings. McLowry sent his horse through the leaping shadows, knowing he had to make a swift decision. Clem Sanderson came out from behind his horse. He had dismounted, or fallen off, and seemed bemused by events. In his confused state he swung his rifle on McLowry, who promptly batted it aside.

"Take it easy, Clem. Where's the rest of them?"

For answer, a horse minced out of the darkness with Marty Eagen bent across the saddle-horn. "I'm all right," he sang out. "But Dobe went down . . . "

"I'm here," Dobe Jenkins panted as he emerged from the murk on foot. "They shot my nag out from under me. Is that Calkin over there?"

"It was," McLowry flung back grimly. "Look, there's a loose horse, Dobe. Go catch it."

The beast had belonged to one of the Collins riders and it tried to duck clear, but Marty Eagen spurred after it, his lariat whirling and then looping through the air like a live thing. He was swallowed in the darkness for a space, but soon returned leading the animal.

"Get aboard, you tub of lard," he told Dobe. "And don't let that one toss you."

"Why, you — "

"Easy," McLowry said sharply. He was thinking of Nate Bream now.

None of the others knew where Nate was. And, just when he was wondering what to do, Bream swept towards them, six-shooter swinging. Nate gestured towards the Split C headquarters squatting at the bottom of the hollow.

"We haven't got much time left, Frank," he mouthed hoarsely. "There's enough men yelling and bellering down there to catch us flat-footed if we don't make tracks *pronto*."

"Clem," McLowry called in to the rancher, "do you want to hit the trail home with the boys?"

"Hell no! If anybody wants to — "

"I reckon I'd better go, Boss," Bream informed him apologetically. "If I stay I'll just — hold — you — up."

McLowry stared in disbelief as the cowhand keeled over in his saddle and tumbled out of leather. His horse dashed off, dragging Bream's left boot in the stirrup.

"Damn it, he's wounded!"

McLowry went after the bobbing

figures of men and horse. Somebody shouted down in the hollow and guns began banging. McLowry caught up with Bream's runaway and clawed at the bridle. He brought out his jack-knife and slashed through the strap. Bream slumped to the earth like a sack of grain.

McLowry leaped to the ground and bent over him, seeing a ragged chest wound. "Why in blazes didn't you sing out at once you were hurt, Nate?" he groaned.

"I didn't . . . I — "

The cowhand sagged back on the turf, coughed a couple of times, and died.

Clem Sanderson had come alongside McLowry. "Is he bad hurt, Frank?"

"He's dead," McLowry whispered brokenly. "Look, Clem, you take Marty and Dobe, and vamoose."

"Too late," Sanderson retorted. "Here they come . . . Scatter, boys!"

Sanderson's prancing horse took him off into the shadows. McLowry held tight to the reins of his own horse and, still on one knee beside the body of Nate Bream, he reloaded his six-shooter and emptied it at the advancing riders. Sanderson and the others returned the fire being poured at them by Marve Collins' hardcases.

McLowry squinted through the deep gloom, seeing horsemen bobbing and wheeling. One of the approaching mounts squealed, went down with its rider sailing over its head. This appeared to make the Split C men more cautious. They could only guess at the location of the scattered Anvil crew and were firing for the most part at random.

Anvil guns boomed back at them. Hooves clashed and thudded. The night was full of belching smoke, crimson flashes and reeking cordite. Harsh calls and cries and curses punctuated the gunfire. For a moment McLowry feared he had been spotted, hunkered there and dragging on the black's reins. But then the Collins riders angled off on his left where Clem Sanderson, Marty Eagen and Dobe Jenkins were playing a deadly game of hide and seek.

As soon as McLowry realised there was an opening that would give him access to the ranch buildings down yonder he swung into his saddle. With a final look at Nate Bream, he sent the black tearing down the slope and veered off to the right of the ranch-house.

But as luck would have it, one of the Collins men spotted him and sent his horse racing to cut him off. The fellow sang out a challenge, and when McLowry kept going two bullets were driven at him. McLowry returned the fire until the hammer of his Colt fell on empty chambers.

The Collins man remained mounted and continued firing. More, he was drawing closer with each passing second. There was just one thing left for McLowry to do. He sent the black horse tearing on for another twenty yards, then drew down hard on the reins. The horse skidded and floundered but stayed upright, and as soon as it had settled Frank raised the rifle he had snatched from his saddle-boot and jacked a shell to the breech. The rifle boomed and the Split C hand screamed and streaked high in his stirrups before bending like a branch in a storm and pitching into the black void of the night.

McLowry paused for only split seconds, listening to the racket up there on the ridge. He was unprepared for the Split C man's loose horse continuing its momentum, and he was obliged to haul his own mount aside to avoid it. Even so, massive body smashed into massive body, and the black was sent into a sickening spin. Try as he did to hold on, McLowry struck the ground and was knocked breathless. Hooves lashed around him in a menacing melee. He rolled wildly and found his feet, albeit groggily, pulled a deep draught of air to his lungs. He had just managed to steady himself when he glimpsed another horseman bearing down on him.

He had lost his rifle in the fall and began a frantic search to recover it. The second Split C rider hammered closer, and when he was only yards off his revolver thundered spitefully. McLowry threw himself forward and went into another roll while bullets slammed into the earth around him. The mounted horse came rushing in, its rider a black, monstrous shape limned against the star-flecked sky. He could see McLowry clearly and he was laughing as he swooped to bring his gun on a level with Frank's head.

"Here goes nothing, you bastard," he bellowed. Just as McLowry gambled all on a wild throw of the dice.

He lunged from his knees and snatched for that gun-hand. He missed, but managed to claw at the down-reaching arm, felt the searing rasp of metal on his wrist. And then he was being dragged along on his stomach. He heaved and the horseman bellowed a curse, trying desperately to free himself. But McLowry had no intention of letting go. The struggling rider was suddenly whipped from his saddle as his mount whirled out from beneath him. He hit the earth, yelping in dismay, and then McLowry sprang like a cougar.

The man was thick-bodied and strong. His breath wheezed through his teeth. He tried to grab the gun at his hip, but McLowry drove an elbow into his face and succeeded in propelling him backwards. The man recovered quickly and bounded to his feet, drawing his revolver at the same time. He triggered, and fire scorched McLowry's face, momentarily blinding him. McLowry's right hand streaked to the jack-knife he had used to free Nate Bream and, as his adversary surged forward, he drove the blade into his stomach. Still the Split C man attempted to fight on, keeping up a stream of garbled vituperation all the while. Then he coughed, shuddered, and sank down in a heap.

McLowry stood up, chest heaving, legs trembling, salt sweat coursing down his face. Away out on his left, horses continued to run and spin and whistle. Gunfire crackled, and then ceased quite abruptly, only to resume a few seconds later. He flung the bloodied knife away and stumbled to where he judged his rifle had fallen. He failed to find it. His six-shooter was gone from its pouch, and he was obliged to return to the dead man and appropriate the weapon that had lately been turned on him.

He had plenty of .45 stuff in his belt and he punched loads into the six empty chambers. He looked around him, wondering where his horse was, wondering, too, what had happened to Clem Sanderson and the others.

A sudden pounding of hooves preceded the emergence of two riders from the gloom, and McLowry flung himself quickly to the ground. The riders halted a few yards away and he picked up part of a garbled exchange.

" . . . damned outfit is all busted to hell, Peck. Mark my words. And who'd have guessed that old buzzard Sanderson had the guts?"

"Yeah," the other grunted. "And Marve's going to have some explaining to do to the law. This could ruin him when it gets out."

"Say, Peck, what do you figure he's going to do with that girl? I don't like that a bit."

"Me neither. He reckons he'll throw a scare into Sanderson to get him to do what he wants."

They spurred away towards a clump of trees and soon vanished from McLowry's sight. McLowry's brow was as dark as thunder. "What does that coyote intend doing with Jenny?" he groaned. "Where is he keeping her?"

A rattle of rifle fire caused him to jerk around and face the south. It was evident that the Split C riders had long since beaten off Clem Sanderson and his two surviving cowhands. There was a lot of shouting away off yonder. Hoofbeats contrived a continuous drumming noise. Closing in on the huddle of buildings that marked the Collins headquarters, McLowry looked across at the barn, hesitated for a moment to test the shadows, then hurried towards the building.

He reached the end facing the east without mishap and hugged the ground when someone appeared at the back of the ranch-house. He watched a stooped form shuffle past and tried to pick up what the man was muttering to himself. On the spur of the moment he yielded to a crazy impulse.

"Who's that?" he challenged in a sibilant whisper.

"Huh?" the other exclaimed, halting in his tracks. "Who are *you*? What do you want?"

For all the man's boldness, McLowry could see that he was thoroughly frightened. He said in the same low voice: "Come over here."

He read age in the shadowed features that were presently turned towards him.

The old fellow started to back-track, but froze when McLowry told him to hold on. "Just want a couple of words with you, Pop."

"Brin sent me to get his horse ready. I got to do what Brin tells me, mister."

"I know Brin sent you," McLowry said and raised a finger to his lips. "But there's one of Sanderson's bunch hiding out in the barn. Come over here quick."

McLowry heard him sucking his breath between his teeth. He squinted this way and that, peered back at the house.

"You dead sure?" he gulped.

"Dead sure. I want you to take a message back to Brin."

That sucking noise again. Then: "I don't know you. Who are you?"

"Boss told me to watch this end in case that Anvil crowd got close enough to start a fire maybe," McLowry explained.

The old-timer wheeled away suddenly and McLowry grabbed him, locking an arm round his throat.

"You make one little cheep, Pop, and I guess I'll have to break your neck. *Sabe?*"

"What — what do you want? I never done nothing . . . "

"Nobody said you did. I just want to know where the girl is, Clem Sanderson's daughter."

"But I — I don't know where she's at."

"The hell you don't! I hate having to hurt you, Pop, but you're asking for it. One squeeze and your neck'll crack like a piece of stick."

"No — no . . . Don't mister. I'll tell you. See — see that room at the back? There's a light . . . "

"Are you telling the truth, old-timer? Because, if you're not — "

"I swear that's where she is. But you'd better — "

McLowry had heard enough. As he had said, he didn't like having to harm the old fellow, but he had to ensure that he kept his mouth shut for a while. A crisp clip behind the ear with the barrel of his gun produced a low groan, and he gripped the old-timer before he fell and dragged him into the gloomy barn.

He emerged and looked along the rear of the main building. He hugged the pools of inky shadow until he reached the back porch. He straddled the railing and peered at the lighted window the old fellow had spoken of.

A burst of shooting broke out at the front of the house, and was answered by gunfire in the distance. It indicated only one thing to McLowry: Clem Sanderson had no intention of clearing out without his daughter. Clem, Dobe and Marty were intent on working in again, harassing the Split C crew, and hoping perhaps that the tactics would give Frank McLowry a better chance to search for Jenny.

McLowry crept past the back door of the ranch-house. There was a smell of flowers in the air here that struck an incongruous note, considering the circumstances. Roses. They clung to the railing of the porch, wreathed about it in profusion. Now he was below the lighted window itself, and he dropped down to watch and listen.

Inside the house, a clock commenced chiming, each musical peal causing his nerves to jump. He tried to control the jittery feeling. If he were to be caught here, nothing would save him. If the oldster in the barn came round and raised the alarm it would spoil everything. If he failed to rescue Jenny, nothing else would matter much, in any case.

If, if, if!

He risked lifting his head, his eyes narrowing when he noticed a chink in the curtains. He tried squinting from every angle, trying to get a better look into the room. Then something moved into his field of vision, a short, blocky figure. The man was bare-headed, and when he turned, McLowry was able to see the dark, hawk-like features. Brin

Eckols! So Eckols had been chosen to guard Jenny.

McLowry's fingers closed on the gun he had taken from the dead Split C man. It lacked the comfortable, familiar feel of his own six-shooter, but it gave him confidence, nevertheless. If only he could catch a glimpse of Jenny to assure himself she was all right . . .

Eckols was speaking now, smiling a little in as much as a bird of prey can smile. His words drifted out in an unintelligible, muffled drone. McLowry saw the foreman frown suddenly in annoyance. He was convinced by then that Eckols was speaking to Jenny. He craned his neck again, but without any more success.

Then Eckols crossed the room and opened a door, and McLowry's heart jumped. A stroke of luck? That remained to be seen. The Split C foreman left the room and closed the door behind him, and McLowry knew he could wait no longer.

He tapped on the window pane

and long seconds plodded by during which nothing happened. He swore in frustration, tapped yet again, much harder this time. He held his breath when a shadow approached and an end of the curtain was lifted. Then he saw Jenny, pale, her hair a loose cloud scattered about her shoulders. He pressed his face to the glass so that she would recognise him, saw her eyes widen and shine with hope.

He signalled wildly and she understood. She began wrestling mightily with the windows, straining upwards, and McLowry gripped the outer edge and heaved. The window opened a couple of inches.

"Hurry," he urged. "Do hurry, girl . . . "

"Oh, Frank, I never thought I'd see you again. Marve must be crazy. He intended keeping me here until dad signs over the ranch to him."

"Quiet!" he hissed, hearing the door leading to the porch swing open. A man came through and looked towards the barn. Brin Eckols.

"Where in hell are you, Tom?" he roared.

He stood for a minute, muttering angrily. He jerked and swore when a fusillade of shots far up the hollow crashed through the uneasy silence. McLowry gnawed his lip when Eckols stamped into the yard and started for the barn.

"Keep quiet till I get back," McLowry whispered to Jenny.

He knew what was about to happen. The foreman would discover the man called Tom and learn of the intruder.

McLowry vaulted the porch railing and wormed his way to the barn. He reached the gateway just as Brin Eckols was bending over the man he had knocked unconscious.

"What's wrong, Tom?" Eckols demanded anxiously. "What happened?"

The old fellow sat up, confused, rubbing his head and looking all around him. The foreman gripped his shoulder and gave him a hard shake. Then Eckols seemed to hear something behind him and swung about. McLowry dropped to his haunches in the gloom that cloaked the area surrounding the gateway.

The foreman came to the opening and looked out, revolver at the ready. "Who's there?" he queried tautly.

McLowry levelled his own Colt. "It's Frank McLowry, Brin. I can see you, but you can't see me."

"I can hear you, damn it!"

Before he had finished speaking, Eckols' revolver spat a long lance of flame. The bullet struck the railing of the porch over yonder and spent itself in the darkness. McLowry triggered his gun just as Eckols, realizing that he had missed and that he really was a clear target, broke. He sucked breath noisily and lurched up on his toes, then crumpled down in the straw and mire.

The old-timer had gained his feet by then and was lumbering off towards the corner of the main buildings, yelling blue murder as he went.

McLowry raised his revolver, aimed, then lowered the weapon. It simply wasn't worth while killing the old-timer. He went to where Brin Eckols lay, clawing at his chest, his breathing a hoarse hustle in his throat. McLowry dipped the barrel of his Colt.

"You're dying, mister," he said. "Anything I can do for you?"

"A drink . . . Get me a drink. Whisky, water, anything. Don't matter a damn . . . "

"Who killed Emmet?" McLowry whispered into his face. "Tell me and I'll fetch help."

"You'll never — leave here — alive," Eckols said with a savage, tortured grin. "So it don't matter what you hear. It was Deke who done for your brother. But Calkin just done what — Marve — told him . . . "

His voice tailed off and he shuddered convulsively before dropping back, wide eyes mocking Frank McLowry until they froze in death.

McLowry heard hoofbeats far off

to the south. He heard the man called Tom still yelling; he seemed to be running around aimlessly in the darkness. McLowry spun into the shadows, clambered on to the back porch once more. The rear door hung open, emitting a blade of light. Gun at the ready, he went inside, found himself in a small kitchen where a pot simmered unconcernedly on the stove. A doorway ran off the kitchen and he slipped through. He was in a hallway now which, in spite of its lavish wall decorations and furnishings, smelled somewhat ancient and mouldy.

He hurried along, the blood leaping in his veins, his trigger-finger curled to open fire at a second's notice. Three doors led off the hall on his right. He picked the middle one, tried the handle, and when the lock remained firm, heaved. The strong woodwork creaked but refused to give. The lock was strong.

"Jenny . . . are you there?"

"Yes, yes! I'm here, Frank. But you'd better be careful."

McLowry cast a quick glance up and down the hall, stood back. He was about to fling himself at the door when boots scraped in from the front of the house. Spur rowels spun dully. A man swore, came into view. He was bare-headed, sweaty, and carried the odour of cordite. Surprise shone in his dancing eyes an instant before he snatched at the revolver tucked in his belt. McLowry pumped two slugs into his midriff before he could get the gun clear. He took a couple of awkward steps, towards McLowry, staggered against the wall, then tilted to the floor and shuddered into stillness.

The thundering hoofbeats were drawing closer to the ranch buildings. Men were shouting, calling. McLowry launched himself at the stubborn door and sent it flying into the room beyond. He almost crashed into a distraught Jenny who immediately threw herself into his arms, laughing hysterically.

"Easy, honey. We've got to get out of here fast. Along the hall and into the kitchen, then out back."

"But, Frank . . . "

"Let's go, woman!"

They clattered through the kitchen and out to the back porch. McLowry grabbed the girl's hand and helped her off the end of the porch. He paused there, listening to the riders who were pouring into the front yard.

"We need horses," he whispered. "Without them we won't stand a chance."

Uproar erupted inside the house. The shouting intensified in strength and volume. Above the tumult rose Marve Collins' strident voice.

"Find them!" he was screaming. "The girl's gone . . . That damned McLowry got her. Where in hell is Brin?"

Jenny would have taken flight had not McLowry held on fiercely. Only just in time. Two men raced from the end of the house and headed for the barn. They were out in a minute and clumped past McLowry and the girl crouched in the thick shadows. They disappeared towards the corral, and then McLowry levered Jenny around the gable to reach the front of the house. Here, six or seven horses were tied at the porch railing. One man stood by the saddle-stock, a burning cigarette in the corner of his mouth.

"We're helping ourselves to a couple of these nags," McLowry hissed in Jenny's ear. "Go when I tell you."

The man whirled at the sound of McLowry's footstep, spoke anxiously. "That you, Boss?"

McLowry's six-gun blasted and the man withered and went down in a driving spin. McLowry scrambled over, helped himself to his revolver. By then Jenny was aboard one of the Split C horses and kicking its flanks wildly. It whistled, reared, and then burst into a gallop. McLowry was helping himself to another horse when someone dashed from the front door and skidded to a halt. McLowry recognized Marve Collins.

"Here, Collins!" he yelled. "This is for you, rat."

The Split C boss was whipping his six-shooter up as McLowry's borrowed weapon spouted crimson. McLowry unleashed three shots, then swung himself into the saddle of the horse he had grabbed. Other Split C men spilled out of the house, from both ends of the building. McLowry spurred the beast into a weaving run, and was soon pounding up the long slope of the hollow. Jenny was making good time and had almost gained the rim of the cup.

She waited for him on the ridge and they thrust into the south, pushing the horses hard for a while, but then easing back when it occurred to McLowry that the Split C had shot its bolt and that Marve Collins' grip on the White River range was broken for ever . . .

★ ★ ★

They were only a few miles from Anvil headquarters when they met a band of men clearing Anvil graze to cross over on to Split C territory. It developed that the group was comprised of Sheriff Dan Bennet, his deputy, and a bunch of townsmen the lawmen had recruited for posse duty to sort out the range feud. They had picked up Clem Sanderson on the way and his two riders, Marty Eagen and Dobe Jenkins.

It transpired that the sheriff had finally felt compelled to investigate Marve Collins and his activities. He had learnt most of what had taken place at Split C from Sanderson. And, after Sanderson had greeted his daughter, and Dan Bennet had listened in amazement to Jenny's story of Collins kidnapping her in order to get her father's promise to sell up, the posse-men continued on their way. But not before McLowry had given his version of events at the Collins ranch.

"Marve dead!" Dan Bennet exclaimed incredulously. "Well, by hell, that's something I find hard to swallow. And I'd better tell you something else, mister," he added in a lower key. "No matter what you think, I was always ready to give Marve and his outfit the benefit of the doubt. So maybe it turned out I was wrong, but I'm not making apologies or excuses."

"Nobody's asking you," McLowry retorted. "But when you sweep out the rest of the trash over there, you might see to it that Clem here and other outfits like his get a fair deal in future."

"You killed Brin Eckols as well, you say? And Brin told you Calkin had killed your brother?"

"Calkin did the dirty work right enough," McLowry agreed. "But he was acting under Collins' orders. You see, Sheriff, Marve really did believe he could get his hands on Clem's place — and grab Clem's daughter at the same time. What would you call a man who'd kidnap a girl and force her and her dad to do something they didn't want to do?"

"Plain damn loco," Jed Deakin grunted in disgust. "Dan, you know what I said all along — "

"Yeah, I know what you said all along," the sheriff growled. "But I was the gent who had to stand out there in the middle."

"It's a pity you boys didn't catch on to all that before Collins took the bit between his teeth. If I'd been in your boots, Sheriff, I'd have . . . "

McLowry was talking to himself. Dan Bennet had broken away abruptly and gestured for the others to get moving also. Clem Sanderson left his laughter to join McLowry.

"We intended riding along with the sheriff and giving him a hand," Sanderson said. "But I guess we'll drift back home now and get on with our own business. Is that all right with you fellas?" he added to Dobe Jenkins and Eagen.

"Anything you say, Boss," Dobe Jenkins nodded. "But we'll have to pick up the boys that got gunned down."

"I'll head along with Dobe, if it's all the same to you, Mr Sanderson, sir," Marty Eagen chipped in.

"Thanks, men," Sanderson said with a heavy nod. "On second thoughts, I'll go with you . . . Frank, do you mind taking Jenny on home?"

"All right, Boss, I'll do that."

They said so long, and then he and Jenny were riding side by side, the way it would always be, he knew.

The dark land stretched out before them, raw and wild, and perhaps still bristling with risks and challenges as yet unknown. There were still some loose ends to be tied up, and first thing in the morning he would have to hunt for his horse. Even so, as far as he was concerned, the shimmering stars up yonder represented in some measure the hope and faith that he and Jenny had in the promise of a brighter tomorrow.

Other titles in the
Linford Western Library:

TOP HAND
Wade Everett

The Broken T was big. But no ranch is big enough to let a man hide from himself.

GUN WOLVES OF LOBO BASIN
Lee Floren

The Feud was a blood debt. When Smoke Talbot found the outlaws who gunned down his folks he aimed to nail their hide to the barn door.

SHOTGUN SHARKEY
Marshall Grover

The westbound coach carrying the indomitable Larry and Stretch headed for a shooting showdown.

FIGHTING RAMROD
Charles N. Heckelmann

Most men would have cut their losses, but Frazer counted the bullets in his guns and said he'd soak the range in blood before he'd give up another inch of what was his.

LONE GUN
Eric Allen

Smoke Blackbird had been away too long. The Lequires had seized the Blackbird farm, forcing the Indians and settlers off, and no one seemed willing to fight! He had to fight alone.

THE THIRD RIDER
Barry Cord

Mel Rawlins wasn't going to let anything stand in his way. His father was murdered, his two brothers gone. Now Mel rode for vengeance.

ARIZONA DRIFTERS
W. C. Tuttle

When drifting Dutton and Lonnie Steelman decide to become partners they find that they have a common enemy in the formidable Thurston brothers.

TOMBSTONE
Matt Braun

Wells Fargo paid Luke Starbuck to outgun the silver-thieving stagecoach gang at Tombstone. Before long Luke can see the only thing bearing fruit in this eldorado will be the gallows tree.

HIGH BORDER RIDERS
Lee Floren

Buckshot McKee and Tortilla Joe cut the trail of a border tough who was running Mexican beef into Texas. They stopped the smuggler in his tracks.

BRETT RANDALL, GAMBLER
E. B. Mann

Larry Day had the choice of running away from the law or of assuming a dead man's place. No matter what he decided he was bound to end up dead.

THE GUNSHARP
William R. Cox

The Eggerleys weren't very smart. They trained their sights on Will Carney and Arizona's biggest blood bath began.

THE DEPUTY OF SAN RIANO
Lawrence A. Keating and
Al. P. Nelson

When a man fell dead from his horse, Ed Grant was spotted riding away from the scene. The deputy sheriff rode out after him and came up against everything from gunfire to dynamite.

FARGO: MASSACRE RIVER
John Benteen

The ambushers up ahead had now blocked the road. Fargo's convoy was a jumble, a perfect target for the insurgents' weapons!

SUNDANCE: DEATH IN THE LAVA
John Benteen

The Modoc's captured the wagon train and its cargo of gold. But now the halfbreed they called Sundance was going after it . . .

HARSH RECKONING
Phil Ketchum

Five years of keeping himself alive in a brutal prison had made Brand tough and careless about who he gunned down . . .

FARGO: PANAMA GOLD
John Benteen

With foreign money behind him, Buckner was going to destroy the Panama Canal before it could be completed. Fargo's job was to stop Buckner.

FARGO: THE SHARPSHOOTERS
John Benteen

The Canfield clan, thirty strong were raising hell in Texas. Fargo was tough enough to hold his own against the whole clan.

PISTOL LAW
Paul Evan Lehman

Lance Jones came back to Mustang for just one thing — revenge! Revenge on the people who had him thrown in jail.

HELL RIDERS
Steve Mensing

Wade Walker's kid brother, Duane, was locked up in the Silver City jail facing a rope at dawn. Wade was a ruthless outlaw, but he was smart, and he had vowed to have his brother out of jail before morning!

DESERT OF THE DAMNED
Nelson Nye

The law was after him for the murder of a marshal — a murder he didn't commit. Breen was after him for revenge — and Breen wouldn't stop at anything . . . blackmail, a frameup . . . or murder.

DAY OF THE COMANCHEROS
Steven C. Lawrence

Their very name struck terror into men's hearts — the Comancheros, a savage army of cutthroats who swept across Texas, leaving behind a bloodstained trail of robbery and murder.

SUNDANCE: SILENT ENEMY
John Benteen

A lone crazed Cheyenne was on a personal war path. They needed to pit one man against one crazed Indian. That man was Sundance.

LASSITER
Jack Slade

Lassiter wasn't the kind of man to listen to reason. Cross him once and he'll hold a grudge for years to come — if he let you live that long.

LAST STAGE TO GOMORRAH
Barry Cord

Jeff Carter, tough ex-riverboat gambler, now had himself a horse ranch that kept him free from gunfights and card games. Until Sturvesant of Wells Fargo showed up.

McALLISTER ON THE COMANCHE CROSSING
Matt Chisholm

The Comanche, McAllister owes them a life — and the trail is soaked with the blood of the men who had tried to outrun them before.

QUICK-TRIGGER COUNTRY
Clem Colt

Turkey Red hooked up with Curly Bill Graham's outlaw crew. But wholesale murder was out of Turk's line, so when range war flared he bucked the whole border gang alone . . .

CAMPAIGNING
Jim Miller

Ambushed on the Santa Fe trail, Sean Callahan is saved by two Indian strangers. But there'll be more lead and arrows flying before the band join Kit Carson against the Comanches.

GUNSLINGER'S RANGE
Jackson Cole

Three escaped convicts are out for revenge. They won't rest until they put a bullet through the head of the dirty snake who locked them behind bars.

RUSTLER'S TRAIL
Lee Floren

Jim Carlin knew he would have to stand up and fight because he had staked his claim right in the middle of Big Ike Outland's best grass.

THE TRUTH ABOUT SNAKE RIDGE
Marshall Grover

The troubleshooters came to San Cristobal to help the needy. For Larry and Stretch the turmoil began with a brawl and then an ambush.

WOLF DOG RANGE
Lee Floren

Will Ardery would stop at nothing, unless something stopped him first — like a bullet from Pete Manly's gun.

DEVIL'S DINERO
Marshall Grover

Plagued by remorse, a rich old reprobate hired the Texas Trouble-shooters to deliver a fortune in greenbacks to each of his victims.

GUNS OF FURY
Ernest Haycox

Dane Starr, alias Dan Smith, wanted to close the door on his past and hang up his guns, but people wouldn't let him.

DONOVAN
Elmer Kelton

Donovan was supposed to be dead. Uncle Joe Vickers had fired off both barrels of a shotgun into the vicious outlaw's face as he was escaping from jail. Now Uncle Joe had been shot — in just the same way.

CODE OF THE GUN
Gordon D. Shirreffs

MacLean came riding home, with saddle tramp written all over him, but sewn in his shirt-lining was an Arizona Ranger's star.

GAMBLER'S GUN LUCK
Brett Austen

Gamblers seldom live long. Parker was a hell of a gambler. It was his life — or his death . . .